David Mulwa

Master and Servant

Longman

Longman Kenya Ltd
P.O. Box 18033
Kenya Commercial Bank Bldg.
(Sixth Floor)
Enterprise Road
Nairobi

Associated companies branches and
representatives throughout the world

First published 1979

Second Impression 1988

ISBN 0 582 64246 9

Published by Longman Kenya Ltd., P.O. Box 18033, Funzi Road, Nairobi
and printed by Metro Forms & Systems Ltd., P.O. Box 52899,
Off Shimo La Tewa Road, Nairobi.

One

A hot afternoon. Not a cloud; not even a wisp of it crosses the sky. I am standing under the eaves of our mud house, looking at a pillar of dust spiralling on the plains from earth to sky and wondering whether Moses would have used *this* for guidance in the desert when I hear murmurs on the path down the hill. Two men are coming up this hill towards our home. One is familiar, so familiar that I wince. Everytime he comes up that hill (which has been very often) and finds me at home without a book or scraps of paper, indicative of a young scholar, in my hands, I get a thorough beating on my buttocks. My father doesn't like to see people sitting down doing nothing or musing. I think that's why he always canes me in order to banish all laziness from that part of the body (which he calls a 'drawback'). 'For', says he in his rare happier moods, 'hard work is the key to wisdom—and wisdom lies here'—(rapping my clean-shaven head with his cane to remind me of that fact)—'Not here!' (caning my buttocks thoroughly to discourage my use of them). The other man is tall and, despite the steep gradient, he insists on walking erect, chin up, and listens to my father's philosophies on hard work as if to say, 'Yes, yes, I thought so. I have heard it all before. Next point!'

I feel terrified and I dive into the house and emerge with an abridged version of our Protestant manual: *The Seven Reasons Why We Won't Co-operate with the Church of Rome*. The writing is rather hilly and as hard to understand as the message behind it, and I can make neither head nor tail of it with so many hard words! (What on earth is 'Sa-c-ra-m-ent'?). However, I put on the air of an outstanding scholar and keep working my mouth the way old grandmother does, even when there's not a morsel of food to chew in her mouth.

At last my father and the stranger arrive. I know they have arrived because I hear the stranger's booming voice: . . . 'As I told you,' and because their army boots make more noise on the pebbles than our neighbour's rickety wheelbarrow. Now they are quiet and my father is saying, 'This here is the boy in question—this son of mine has done extremely well as you yourself see. Seven hundred and seventy-six out of eight hundred—top position.'

'You are right. I told you the boy will go a long way. That's why I'm willing to help.'

I secretly glance at the stranger. He is very tall. Now that he has arrived on flat ground, he has assumed a stooping posture. And he's extremely thin and his eyes are large and in danger of dropping out any minute, like the ripe mangoes in our plantation. I don't like him. He looks a caner of children. My father has always had caners of children for his friends.

'Kituku! Chairs!,' my father raps.

I am wondering whether he's re-christening me with that word or whether I am being introduced, when a cane lands on my head to make me look sharp.

'Chairs. Two. In the house. Right here!' I dash into the house and struggle back with the chairs (they are so heavy) and I find them discussing the manual and the stranger commending my father to God's eternal blessing for teaching me the right way in my youth,

2

for when I grow up I'd be surely bound fast to it.

'Now this thing about *their* holy communion: Is there *any* reason why the priest should drink *all* the wine and the congregation merely eat the bread?' thunders the stranger, his eyes popping out in righteous indignation against this unfairness in the distribution of eatables and drinkables in the House of God at the moment of Grace. But now I have brought the chairs and my father gruffly tells the stranger to sit. 'Now Kyanzo,' continues he, 'you have often heard me talk about Kituku. This is the boy who has walked in his father's footsteps in all things righteous. Not that he should boast and develop a big head with that praise.' (Here he raps my head twice with the cane to discourage any big-headedness).

'No,' assents the stranger. 'Boasting isn't good for young people. I have told you so. It isn't good at all. It *is* bad.'

My father nods to conclude that it is, and continues, . . . 'Not to develop a big head! Now Kyanzo, this is why I have arranged to have him transferred to Kyambe, which I hear is a better primary school where he will receive the best education possible and the best Protestant upbringing possible. That's why I have asked *you* to help me in the way of accommodation.'

'And that's why I am glad to help you,' returns Kyanzo.

'Kituku,' my father says. 'From next week you are transferred to Kyambe Primary. And this man here will be in charge of you. When he is not at home, his servant will be in charge of you. And,' turning to Kyanzo, 'because he will be like a father to you, I expect you to be like a son to him—dutiful, obedient and hard-working. If you misbehave he has *my* permission to cane you.' (I am not very sure, but I think Kyanzo has passed his tongue across his lips, his eyes are blazing and I fear he may be a cannibal. I think he is anticipating caning me. And I am more convinced that he enjoys caning. I am even more apprehensive. But my father is talking.) 'So now get ready. Get your clothes washed and your books *well*-packed. And don't forget your Bible.'

My father never repeats an order. I dash into the house to carry out his instructions.

That's how I first heard of Kyanzo's servant.

*　　*　　*

On the morning of that Sunday, when I was to be transferred to Kyambe School, I woke up earlier than usual. Whatever had made me sleep in my pants, I have never been able to find out to this day. But whatever the reason, I had slept in the only pants I possessed. That night we had supped on porridge and, being full and comfortable inside, I slept soundly. Before cockcrow the following morning I was awakened by my brother, who slept beside me angrily protesting, 'Asii . . . ii . . . si! You have pissed on me!'

So I woke up with my pants fast upon my left side and smelling like our biggest he-goat, made a fire, and sat sideways to dry them before my father woke up. For his part, he thought I had woken up out of enthusiasm for the transfer and commended me upon it, when he had woken up and had said his prayers. I was not to go to Sunday School. The servant was arriving early in the morning and we had forty kilometres of cycling to do that day. But my brother escorted me up to the crossroads, where we were to wait for him. I was rather gloomy then, and strongly believed that if the master was a caner of children, then the servant was also. As I lived those thirty or so minutes, we waited for him, wondering what particular type of cannibal he would turn out to be.

Presently we saw him, coming fast down the road. When he reached where we waited, he stopped but did not get off the bicycle.

'I am looking for Kituku—the boy who was transferred to Kyambe School. Are you him?' he asked my brother. The latter denied it and pointed at me offhandedly with his right thumb.

'I was sent to pick *you* up,' he said, emphasizing the pronoun, whether to show preference to my brother, I never could tell. I handed him my basket, in which there were about thirteen books and a blanket, and after I had waved my brother farewell, we were on our way. The man was not talkative and in an attempt to make him open up, I asked him question after question to which he either grunted by way of acknowledgement or said something midway between a horse's grunt and a donkey's bray; though what message he meant to convey I couldn't make out. In the following silence, we covered quite a distance until a porcupine happened to cross the road, upon which he lessened speed to survey this animal, and asked, 'Animal what you call this?'

'What?' I asked, not believing what I had heard.

'Ears you block with wax? Question I ask; animal what you call this?'

I comprehended and said gratefully, 'Porcupine.'

He spoke with a heavy accent, like a child that was learning a language. The man was not from our part of the colony. Then he reverted into Swahili and said, 'The name's Muhammad. My name. Hamad for short.'

My knowledge of Swahili couldn't measure up to

his but, compared with his knowledge of my language, mine was by far superior. Henceforth Muhammad and I spoke in Swahili, until I lost him.

'And your name is . . . Kituku er . . .'

'Joseph,' I cut in.

He cycled on, uphill and downhill and over flat ground as if carrying a thirty-four kilogram child on the back seat was as normal as breathing the very air around him. After my name he did not ask me another question and I had time to survey him. He was tall and very broad-shouldered, this width thinning out to a narrow waist so that he looked to me like an enormous wasp sitting upright. He had a rather slanting head from the top to the base of a neck which was about three times the size of mine. His arms were rather too long and seemed all muscle. Considering the ease with which he cycled, I concluded he must be a very strong man, a fact which didn't deceive me.

We rounded a bend and came to a shopping centre that boasted about ten buildings and a large square at the centre, which, as I later observed, was always crowded on market days. About half a kilometre from the shopping centre, we branched into a side road that went slightly uphill. Above us, the peaks of the hills towered and were thickly forested as far as I could see. As we went up, the vegetation grew thicker, the grass grew taller, and soon we passed large tracts of gum and eucalyptus trees. Suddenly it was cool and I found myself planning to stay here all my life and never go back home. As if to echo my thoughts, Hamad said, 'That's home across there.'

There were only two houses. One was an immense structure, whose walls were half-built and whose roof had only a few iron sheets to its credit. Men were working around this house and their shouts and hammering reached me distinctly, despite the perpetual rustling of eucalyptus leaves in the wind. The other house was built just beyond the big one. This one was grass-thatched but I could not see its walls because it was built on the side of the hillock. Beyond the house a thick forest stretched out to the hills far, far above. It was altogether a most pleasant sight and I felt a strong urge to plunge into the forest and explore what lay within it.

At length we reached the main house before which we alighted. As we arrived the six or seven builders looked up and all activity abruptly stopped. Then, just as suddenly, the men came to life again and crowded around in a body, laughing, gesticulating and calling, 'Hamad!' Soon hands were shaking and mouths were smiling. A young man offered to carry my basket to the house when the others clamoured around Hamad. Not being very much acquainted with this boisterousness (what with the cane and the Protestant manual), I was obliged to stand aside and stare and pretend to grin and laugh and, in short, teach the chameleon his trade. And now I had time to survey my host. He was not particularly handsome of face. It was rather large with a broad dilated nose that seemed to be always smelling some evil through one nostril and blowing it out through the other. Below the flaring nose was a wide mouth and thick lips. But what was most striking about him were his eyes, whose whites were a bright white, emphasizing the dark pupils so that he seemed to pierce right through whatever he happened to be looking at. But it was fascinating to see him talk to the men and bestow upon each of them that flashing smile, betraying white, even, teeth. He was shorter than at least three of the men assembled there, but such was the manner in which he carried his shoulders that he seemed to be always squaring up for a fight or ready to pounce on something, giving him an air of immense strength that dwarfed all the others.

Once, my grandmother told me the story of the genie that had come to the village and stolen a child. Looking at this man, I couldn't help recalling this story. He seemed to be a creature I knew very well and yet one that was, like the forest, dark and unknowable. But now he was walking towards the mud-and-grass-thatch-house, beckoning me to follow him.

Inside, the hut was rather congested, with utensils lying about the floor. On one wall was a button of a window below which was a wooden bed. In one corner were a number of boxes and an odd assortment of clothes. In the other corner an ill-made and much used guitar was propped against the wall. At the centre of the hut, a pole stretched up to the roof supporting the hut, and beside the pole, a hearth made of three stones had been constructed. All these I saw as I entered the hut. Now I began to look for signs of the owners of the house—especially Kyanzo of whom I thought with dread. Fixing those eyes on me Hamad seemed to decipher what I was thinking for he said, 'They are not here. Master and his wife and child are home. They won't come till harvest time.'

I was greatly relieved. Harvest was two and a half seasons off!

'Where is home?'

'A long way away. Three hundred and twenty kilometres, so they say.'

That was all I learned about the whereabouts of my hosts and, for many days, I tried to establish their exact geographical location. Many a time, when I was

8

well settled in Kyambe School, I would take a pair of compasses and, taking two and a half centimetres to represent one hundred and sixty kilometres, I would measure out three hundred and twenty kilometres and scan the whole area within this radius in search of my dreaded hosts, especially Kyanzo.

At one point, the compass hit the centre of a large lake, and I was seized with fear and then hope that they were drowned in there and would never come back. Again, I was told they were camped on the peak of the most rugged hill in the whole neighbourhood, and I was at great pains to know what they were doing up there, whether they had carried enough ropes with them and how they would come down the precipice if they hadn't.

'Hungry? Eh, little man?' Hamad said, picking me up and placing me on the bed as if I was a mere infant. I said that I was, and then Hamad began rummaging among the utensils from among which he fished out a half-used packet of maize meal. Then he set about making the fire, which smoked very heavily and, since all the smoke was going out through the little hole behind me and was likely to suffocate me, I began to cough and protest involuntarily, whereupon Hamad advised me to go out, get some fresh air and look about me.

The hut was built a few metres from the brook that ran from the hills far above us, down to the great murmuring river about a kilometre below the hut. Across the brook, the forest stretched from its bank to the hilltops as I have said before. And in the brook, the water rippled incessantly cold, clear and unblemished. I sat down on the brook-bank and dangled my feet into a clear pool, watching the bubbles sail across the surface of the pool around my

9

shins and over the mini-waterfall further downstream. A slight wind was rising.

How long I sat here I do not know, for I did not care about time. I felt immensely relieved and free. No more my father's sharp commanding voice, no more caning, the forced prayers of morning before I woke up, after breakfast, the prayers before each task, the prayers before lunch and before and after dinner, the prayers for the Monarch over the sea that she may long reign over us, the prayers for the White people who had brought us light to banish all our darkness; for *their* government, that it may continue to look kindly down upon us; for those ill-advised rebels who were rising in discontent against *that* government and killing people indiscriminately—so that the light of God may descend upon *them* too. Then there had been prayers for the family (in which each one of us was singled out, merited and demerited, castigated and consecrated). No more the Bible lessons in which the commandment, 'Children, obey your parents, for this is right', was always twirled around the cane, and strengthened by the words of the preacher, 'He who denies his child the rod hates his child'; lessons in which my father took great delight. Here I was free to let my mind wander without an assault upon my buttocks. Here I didn't care whether I was a Roman or a Roman Catholic or a Protestant, a pagan, or one of those 'barbarous' Moslems my father would never talk about without raising his voice in anger. I began to wonder what my host's child looked like and whether it was a boy or a girl, whether his wife was as tall and lean as he was, and whether she had equal authority to scare and banish all my senses with the cane acting as servant, whether she held the Protestant manual to her bosom

10

as firmly as did my mother on my father's orders. In short, my mind ran through practically all the evils known to its childish state and which had made my life and the lives of all my loved ones turbulent, miserable and far from the simplicity and peace emitted by this brook.

At length I rose and followed the brook downstream until, after a short distance, I came upon a garden that stretched down to the river bank. This was a marvel of bench terraces, with still greater marvels of deep trenches dug at the top of each terrace. These trenches were planted with bananas and various fruit trees. But the terraces were empty and seemed to be under preparation for planting. I was marvelling at the hands that must have done this work, when Hamad called me and announced that food was ready. At that call I hurried up the hill, determined not to give him offence.

He had made thick porridge and some kind of mashed tomato soup, seasoned with pepper and salt. I didn't feel particularly happy about this dish. But as this was my first day here and I must show proper manners lest Hamad find reason to use the cane, I made the best show of gorging as I possibly could. This late lunch was soon over and Hamad gave me the utensils and pots to wash in the brook, and this task I performed with pleasure. I had not washed the second plate before I heard the sound of singing and a guitar accompanying. And the singer had not sung half the stanza before all the builders laid down their tools and made for the hut. Thus, eager to see what went on, I hurried over my cleaning and returned to the hut.

No one took any notice of me when the clanging of plates, spoons and pots announced my entry. No one took any notice of me when I put these down with great trembling of the hands, or when pots, plates and spoons tumbled off the stack which I was trying to build. All the seven pairs of eyes were glued upon Hamad's face and upon *his* eyes which were shut, as if to make sure the sweetly sad melody he was playing didn't escape through them. Looking at that face as it passes before my eyes now, I believe that the man who played this music suffered a great deal, that perhaps he shut his eyes lest the tears bubbled up and spilled over, that the breast that heaved as he sang softly, wept instead, and the heart beneath it wept and that his whole being wept tears that seemed to fall through the fingers on to the wires of the old guitar and sprinkled all over into the air we breathed, to give us a touch of his sorrow, the origin of which we did not know. Even to my childish eyes, it was plain to see that behind the flashing smile and behind the dilating nose that seemed to inhale and exhale evil in equal measure, Hamad was a very sad being.

Presently he began to sing and his voice, full and mellow at first, gradually thinned out until it seemed as if the great rugged man of immense power had gradually dissipated and dissolved into a young graceful girl of fifteen. It was a question and answer song in which he sang the stanza in a language we did not understand and the guitar answered him—and not one of us moved or shuffled our feet for it seemed then as it does now, that each of us was in some way involved in that song.

The song came to an end, and out of the politeness implanted in me by my father, I loudly clapped my hands and smiled as widely as I possibly could—an exercise which cost me great exertion, for I did not feel like smiling at that time. Apart from myself, none of the audience clapped. Each was caught by the end of the song in his own posture, in his own sadness, each staring at his own infinity. But on my clap, eyes turned on me, slowly, and hostile and to this day, I still feel the weight of that unspoken condemnation, and still feel guilty.

At length Hamad opened his eyes, looked at us and laughed. But he did not well conceal that lie, for someone asked him what he had been singing about. He turned his eyes on the questioner, but the eyes no longer seemed to pin the questioner to his stool. Now they were slightly bloodshot so that the pupils lost some of their dark colour. They were ordinary bloodshot eyes; and it was a normal voice that replied in ordinary tiredness, 'Oh, nothing really—just a song about some people.'

But in my child's heart, I knew that there was something he did not want to tell us, and I resolved to ask him when I was more certain of him and when I had fully cultivated his confidence. To avoid further questioning, he began to play the guitar again, but this time none of us felt as we had felt when he played the first song. Now he strummed the guitar as if he must make it bend to his will, and he accompanied it with songs both in Swahili and in our language, his singing in the latter being a source of great merriment when he stumbled over irregular words and tried to fit them into the rhythm. And in this way, the evening wore away fast and the men went back to the new house where they kindled a big fire. We sat before it and shared in roasting the meat of the antelope they had killed early that morning. It was altogether a pleasant evening and, holding a meaty rib across my lips as if I must blow as much out of it as my brother used to on his reed pipe, I leaned against the door frame and looked out into the darkness.

The stars above shone unusually bright and I could clearly trace the Milky Way, as it arched like a gigantic bow across the two distant forested peaks far, far above me. The outlines of the mountains cascaded into one another until the farthest end was lost in the dim light. And out of them I heard the sounds of the night. Sometimes the forest rustled in the wind, at other times, a jackal called, a hyena laughed, a fox barked and I was afraid, just as I had been during many nights at home as I waited for the others to come home. But looking at the brown faces illuminated by the fire and hearing the deep confident laughter of those men, I gradually composed myself until the rib had been picked clean and I had thrown it into the night and listened as it whistled through the air and landed with a splash in the brook further down. At length a man called me, and handing me a piece of fat meat, asked whether I was used to starvation where I came from. Every man present seemed to have found a game out of this question and by the time I went to sleep, I still had a piece of meat but I hadn't any energy left to chew it with. And as I lost knowledge of all the world around me, I am sure I heard one of the men say, ' . . . eat it when he wakes up in the night.'

Two

'Wake up!' Hamad was saying.

'Eh?'

'Wake up! It's school today! Have you forgotten?'

14

Yes! I had forgotten and I woke up with a start and to the sound of the Mission School bell.

The sun was up and its bright rays streamed through the ventilation of the hut, making me feel guilty of oversleeping on my first day to Kyambe School. For a moment I was under the impression that it was sometime in the afternoon and that I was very late and would always be late all my life; that Kyanzo towered many feet above me and eagerly wet his lips, anticipating the moment I jumped out of bed so that he might cane me. So I jumped out of bed and dived into my pants which I had hung on a string above the bed, and bolted out.

Great was my relief when I found that it was only morning, that the bell was only announcing daybreak, that I had at least two hours before parade-time and that I need not panic. So I went back into the hut to find Hamad towering over the pot, in which porridge bubbled. I was going to pick up a piece of soap and go to the brook to wash my face, when he stopped me and asked what I was doing. I told him. He was silent for a while, then: No, I was not to go to the brook; *he* would take me there. He would make sure I was spotlessly clean, for cleanliness was highly emphasized in Kyambe School. Well, that was a big change, from the way things were run at my father's home, and I would not hear of it at first. But so strong was the will of this servant that I couldn't contradict him, even though what he had said was uttered in a low voice. Thus, relieved of the responsibilities of cleaning myself, I set about performing my academic ones. I made sure that any creases in my exercise books were well-flattened out, that each book was properly covered by a new newspaper jacket, that my name appeared in capitals across the top of each book; and that, of course, each book was well-labelled.

I was surveying the results of my handiwork when Hamad called me to the brook for a thorough washing. And a thorough washing it was! He literally made me jump into the pond and then sat me on a stone with my feet dangling into the water as they had done on the day of arrival about a week before. Upon this stone Hamad waited like a good angel with all the required washing materials in his hands. There was a fibre sponge with which he scrubbed me as if to wreak vengeance upon my back. Any left-over marks of dirt or irregularity upon my body met with Hamad's disapproval, when he would throw down the sponge and handle that tender part with the sharp strong nails he had on every finger.

Thus, washed clean, I emerged from the pond, not without some hopes that a voice would waft down upon us from the forest up above and proclaim that the Lord was very pleased with me. We quickly took our breakfast and together set out for school, which was about three kilometres by a road which had been misused and reduced to a mere cattle-track.

The school was built on top of a small hillock at the apex of which a large church-building stood. On top of the church stood a cross, supporting a white angel, who stood there in a frowning attitude, as if he passed judgement upon all those who went in and out of the Lord's house. This angel always seemed in danger of falling off the cross, especially on stormy days which Kyambe location was amply blessed with. Below the church, the small hillock had been rather finely terraced, and upon these terraces stood innumerable houses, some of which I quickly recognized as classrooms and others which were a puzzle to me for many days to come. These were houses on which the labels 'Study', were stuck. And when, one Saturday morning, I walked around the school compound, I was greeted by more and more of these labels which informed me that I was in the house of 'Meditation' or 'Correction' or 'Books' or 'Tools' or 'Shed' or 'Pastor' or 'Sister-assistants' or 'Head-nurse' or 'Kyambe Dispensary' or 'Prayer-room'. It was long before I found some order among these buildings, enough to know that when I was not in the classroom or in the study room, I was supposed to be in either the bookshop or the prayer room. Throughout my stay in Kyambe Primary, I strictly observed this order, lest I be directed to the house of Correction. And throughout my early stay in Kyambe Primary, not a day passed but I expected my father to bolt out of the dark insides of this correction-house, wielding a large cane in the air, seeking me out from among the boys, and proclaiming the headmaster's leave for him to whip my buttocks that my head might grow wiser.

Thus Kyambe School.

When we arrived at the compound, we found quite a number of pupils milling about, talking, joking, idling, waiting for the great wheel of education to get rolling so that they might be tossed and rolled about upon it. We had just come to the first classroom and with Hamad in front of me like my good Angel, we were surveying this building, where I would begin my new intellectual life, when some great hulking devil of a pupil came upon us and asked us what we thought we were doing there. Not knowing any English, Hamad was at a loss and he looked at me for salvation, upon which I answered Gruff's question. Hamad returned in Swahili that 'we' were there for transfer. This he spoke quietly, slowly and with great respect,

17

which seemed out of place for such a fully muscled figure as he was. But this humility and its good intentions were lost on Gruff, who now guffawed that we might as well be apes and how on earth did this ape (meaning Hamad) and this apeling (meaning *me* to my great indignation),—yes how did we even presume to think of joining Kyambe School! After which Gruff placed great attention on Hamad's appearance and remarked that his Maker must have been asleep when He made such a rude patchwork of a face as that before him. What an over-hanging forehead! And what large eyes!—'Blink you fool—Blink!' Gruff would teach him how to blink! Gruff didn't like impertinent new-comers who thought they were somebodies. Did we know *who* Gruff was?—He was the Chief's son, came to school on his *own* motorcycle, and when *he* was tired of that groaner, he would go in for a car! Did we know Gruff? Gruff was the terror of Kyambe School! Reverend Wranglem was afraid of him and thought him the Devil's son. Did we know Gruff? No! But *he* would tell us: the puny headmaster was afraid of *him!* All those cowardly teachers were afraid of him. No prefect dared give him an order. Gruff did what he liked. 'So blink, you fool! Blink!'

By now there was quite a gathering around us and all sorts of names came to our ears. One particularly impertinent little urchin began to take liberties with me and pinch any part of my body that presented itself to him. He dared me to retaliate, encouraged by the congregation. Not wanting to be outdone, Gruff resumed his description of my guide and friend: 'Look at those holes on his nose! Take snuff? eh? Friends, I bet this ape takes snuff!—Nose seems particularly dilated for snuff—is that not so, you savage?

Rough hands! Been digging out squirrels eh?' (Here Gruff shoved Hamad backwards) . . . And look at *that*! (here Gruff was pointing at Hamad's manhood) —Guess Miss (Dash) would like it!' (loud laughter from the congregation) and I wondered who Miss Dash was and why she must like it. 'Use a ruler!' came a suggestion—'No need! it's a very donkey's tail!' Gruff said, 'Let's see!' He *must* pull down Hamad's trousers. And there is cheering and wild support! I hear 'Grandfather greenhorn' repeated. I see Hamad's eyes shine. And I see the nostrils dilate and he is trembling. And I see his hand flash upon Gruff's collar. The next moment Gruff is in the air and then he's falling a few metres away, taking three or four of the retreating boys with him as he falls. No one speaks any more. No one says I am a 'greenhorn' anymore and I feel proud of my protector, who is now moving menacingly towards Gruff who is slinking away along the floor. And now Hamad is sweetly talking in that low voice of his, as if nothing has happened. But I don't understand a single word he says. The language is foreign and he is talking in a thin voice like a woman.

At that moment, the bell rang and as if heralded, the headmaster appeared. I knew he was the headmaster because there was a general pandemonium and fleeing, accompanied with hen-clucks of, 'The headmaster, The headmaster!' Only Gruff, three boys, Hamad and myself, remained. Looking at this person of Authority and Intelligence, I was afraid that we were in for trouble, that the chief and his askari contingent would be here any minute, and that I would spend all my life in prison and die a 'greenhorn' there. In a moment I was disabused however, when the headmaster said he had seen everything and, turning to Gruff and the three boys, ordered that they present themselves at 'Correction' where he should find them with pants down—at which I saw the three boys glance at the cane in the headmaster's hand and wince. He then introduced himself in English and said he was Johannes Mathayo and asked what he could do for us. When I had explained who we were and what had brought us there, I saw him nod knowingly. Then he told me to go into his office and wait for him there. Without any ceremony he left us and I watched him walk from classroom to classroom in the most brisk manner I had ever seen. And wherever he went, the boys snapped to attention and, upon his departure, worked with such frenzy that I wondered whether he had shed some madness off his coat and bequeathed it to them. He was a short, brown, thin man, on whose face was a most disproportionate quantity of beard and moustache. He was rather shabby, in an old black suit that didn't seem to fit and which looked as if it had been slept in. To this was added a tie that was so old-looking and twisted that I entertained thoughts of it having been used to tether goats.

Such was the figure that terrorised everyone and which commanded me to wait upon its leisure. Hamad declined the official invitation and, handing me the documents that the headmaster of my former school had given my father as my testimonials, he said that he would see me at lunchtime. He added that I should not tolerate any rude boys, that I only needed to report them to him and he would give them fair treatment and that I was to work hard—for that was his employer's (and my host's) wish.

Having thus delivered himself, he left, and I was left standing in the great school courtyard, looking

20

at him as he descended the hill until he was hidden by clusters of forest far below the school. To my childish and imaginative mind, he seemed to be going down, down into his grave, and without any apparent reason I was sad, and my heart was weeping as if he was truly dead.

I turned my back upon that sight in search of the office. But I could not locate it. Nor was there anyone about that I could ask. Everyone seemed to be running about their tasks as if their lives literally depended upon speed. I thus decided to remain in the courtyard until such time that the fear of my headmaster was less upon the boys, and to enquire about the office at a pupil's leisure. Since it was still cold and I needed some exercise I began to walk around the courtyard, noting the classrooms that enclosed it. And I walked around that courtyard so many times that by the time the headmaster made me stop, I had known that the circumference of the courtyard was exactly two hundred and thirteen steps plus both my left and right feet joined together. But the greatest discovery I made was a large yellow board posted above the door of the Standard Six Classroom telling me:

IN THIS SCHOOL YOU MUST SPEAK ENGLISH

In front of this stern commandment there was a facial representation of a happy Kyambe youth who had been a steady English speaker and who now grinned from ear to ear and displayed a set of very white teeth. From his mouth proceeded stars of English words, which stars exploded everywhere about him and led up to a galaxy in the blue heavens, from where a broad bright shaft of light descended, as if through the English language, the bliss of eternity was sure to fall upon him.

Below this commandment and its defender, there was the warning:

AVOID VERNACULAR IT MAKES YOU STUPID.

Under this second caption were two pictures: the left one showed a dark black youth, his tears perpetually falling in a pool on the ground below him while he was forever engaged in fending off the headmaster's cane that always hovered above his head. Beside him was another black elderly man who bore a huge hunchback of all troubles attendant upon all Vernacular Specialists, and was undergoing the last afflictions of hunger, and had his chin in his hands. His eyes popped out in perplexity and stared into dark oblivion making the old man seem devoid of all hope. And around both of these creatures was immense darkness that had no star within it and which enveloped these two stupid generations.

'Well?' cracked a voice just above my ear as I stood looking at the commandments. I jumped bodily and would have collided with the headmaster had he not anticipated this move, no doubt having experienced this stupid phenomenon innumerable times before.

'Why aren't *you* in my office?' he rasped.

'I don't know where it is, I replied.

'I don't know where it is—*Sir*!' he repeated after me and hit my head when he came to that honorary title. Not knowing whether he was mocking or correcting me, I kept quiet as a safeguard against making mistakes.

'*I don't know where it is—Sir*,' he repeated, this time emphasizing each word with a rap of the cane and doubly emphasizing the last one. Once I had seen my father break in our dog that had been the terror of both home and neighbourhood.

dog into a snare and everytime he

occasioning yowls which made

mother sniff with grief—and every

would dangle a piece of meat jus

Then he would say, 'Come here,' and

closer. He would then snap his finger

here,' and the dog would then get it piece of meat.
After months and months of this treatment which
reduced the dog to a most pitiable skeleton, it was
taken out of the trap and told to, 'Come here.' A
great lamentable change had come over it. Everytime
my father snapped his fingers, the dog would come to
him, wagging its tail in gratitude and making amends
for I-don't-know-what. Everytime we took the cattle
to the pastures the dog would meekly follow at my
father's heels, never barked and was about as useful
in the herdsman's profession as the grass that lay
rotting upon the surface on the red earth. Now our
home was quiet. No more the deep barks that re-
sounded off the cliffs across the river; no more the
growls that kept all suspicious visitors at bay until we
would license them into the compound. It was now a
quiet home of no noise, except when father was
drumming the good qualities of the Protestant
manual into some erring offspring . . .

Now as the headmaster introduced me to the
mono-syllable: *Sir*, I thought about our dog and
wondered what course of action it was possible to
take, considering my diminutive frame and intellect,
against this learned and hardened headmaster.

He now had both my arms in his right hand and
was dragging me along the courtyard and to the back
of Classroom Six, through a gap between Standard
Six and Seven classrooms. When we had paced along

...rk crevice, Headmaster Mathayo pushed me ...into the open and said, 'That's my office!'

The object he indicated, was a house, the back of which bordered the forest and above which, the tall eucalyptus trees rustled in the wind, like the fallen angels that had cried themselves hoarse.

It was built on a lower terrace than the one that housed the classrooms and on which we now stood. The two terraces were connected by cemented steps— down which I was propelled, thrust into the sober office and seated on a bench to the immediate left of the door. Here I was to sit and wait, so said the head-master. I was not to touch anything; was not to look at the pictures of the woman directly opposite me; was to fold my hands and books on my lap and employ all my faculties in contemplating them. With these directions, Headmaster Mathayo closed the door upon both me and the strange white woman who (much against my will) stared at me through the glass frame. And I wondered why her hair was so long and why it glittered on one side only, as if that patch would fly off the head any minute now and flutter about my eyes, why her neck was so long and what was that upon her neck. There were some words below the picture but I did dare not stand to look. At this moment, a small branch fell off the trees above and caused such a loud sound on the iron roof that I nearly jumped off the bench. Long afterwards I was still convinced that it had been a messenger, sent to confirm the order that I was not to look at anything— especially this strange woman. And when the terror had subsided and my eyes were fast upon my books and hands again, I still had the strange feeling that this woman was looking at me, was saying I must not look at her, must obey the headmaster's command to

24

the letter and must speak English so that I might reach the stars. Up and above, the eucalyptus trees sang on in the wind, and their sigh wafted into this room like so many broken 'Amens' in a funeral oration. As I sat there, waiting to be officially transferred to Kyambe School, my mind slowly drifted to Hamad and I wondered what *he* would do under these circumstances.

At length, I heard footsteps on the staircase and I sat bolt upright, hands and books on my lap, and cut a very ridiculous figure indeed, until the headmaster re-entered and reprimanded me for not standing up to acknowledge his presence as my superior.

After this reprimand, Headmaster Mathayo stormed to the back of his desk, sat down and pulled the chair behind him with such squeakings, that my ears hurt and I winced. Then he poked his forefinger at me and ordered me to give him any documents I possessed. He pored over them as if they were police records of all the crimes I had committed and he expected to unearth the basic monstrous crime and punish me for it. At length he laid the papers aside and fixed his bloodshot eyes upon me, before which eyes I squirmed and shifted and a-hemmed and trembled. He seemed to enjoy it, for when I looked at him, I found him smiling like an old ogre ready to devour me. Then he began to ask innumerable questions designed to confirm the information he had read and to make all my senses and confidence flee. Thus I was asked whether I was *really* Kituku? 'Yes, sir—Christened Joseph? Yes, sir!—Not on account of day-dreaming I hope? No, sir! Christian? Yes, sir!—Father and mother Christian? Yes, sir!—Of the Protestant Faith? Yes, sir—Good. Now then, you wanted to transfer to Kyambe School?—Yes, sir.—Why?

This question utterly confounded me. In all my preparations and consequent stay with Hamad, I had never asked myself the reason why. Everything relating to my schooling and to this transfer, had been arranged by my father and I was not supposed or expected to delve into parental motives especially when those were bound up with Ephesians Six, where obedience was paramount, and sprinkled and spiced with both the whole Book of Laws and Commandments and the Protestant manual. I trembled and said that my father had heard good reports of its being a good Protestant school—which answer seemed to satisfy the scowling giant before me and he said, 'Good! Now look here . . .'

And he went on telling me about the great merits, fame and good repute of Kyambe Primary from religious ones, (it being a Protestant Missionary School) to educational ones and crowned these praises with an observation that no boy ever failed in Kyambe Primary and that I should consider myself lucky and be forever grateful. After this, we delved into the narrow and intricate pathways of school rules, religious rules, academic rules, hygienic rules and, in short I was so harassed by the rules of Kyambe School, that I didn't make any movement without being conscious that there was some rule against it. And by the end of that day, when I was at last free to go home to Hamad I felt as if I was carrying a huge placard with the inscription 'THOROUGHLY RULED' on my back, where it had been nailed to keep it fast and secure.

Having ensured my good conduct in Kyambe by his catalogue of laws, rules and commandments, the headmaster propelled me before him, out into the compound, to introduce me to the school, which was then on parade.

There were over three hundred pupils in that parade, all looking clean in pressed khaki pants and shirts, hair cropped close to the skull, arms held stiffly down the sides, palms clasping the pants as if the latter would drop any minute. Each class paraded before its own classroom, the doors of which stood open, like mouths that had expelled constipating gut-material and were glad to have done it. At the other end of the rectangular court yard, the eight or so teachers and six sober-looking prefects stood stiffly to attention. It was a spectacle that suggested great discipline which any army general would have been proud of.

To this spectacle, we made our appearance, I in my ridiculous poise and the headmaster in his triumphant one, as he now pulled me along with him as if I was a prisoner brought before a Court Martial. As we entered, the School Captain snapped, 'Atten-shun!' and the whole school went to such heights of attention that I wondered how the heads managed to stand upon those stiff necks without the eyes popping clean out into the air. And in this attitude, I was dragged to the front where the headmaster let go of me, and made me extremely nervous.

At the centre of the courtyard was a flagpole and beside it and holding a flag, stood a most un ually disciplined schoolboy whose only difference with the flagpost was that he had two legs to his credit and the post had none. My attention to this figure was roused when, upon the captain's roar of 'God save the Queen' and the whole school singing this anthem, the bundle of flag began to glide up the post trying to make sure that it kept in rhythm with the music below it, till it reached the top where it was unfurled, to the great satisfaction of all present that God would surely save the Queen, make her glorious, make her to long reign over us et cetera, et cetera. The specimen of discipline now secured the flag, walked backwards, faced the flag with satisfaction, stamped both his legs like an impatient he-goat at the sight of an insoluble mystery, saluted and marched with a soldierly stiffness back to the Standard Seven ranks.

The headmaster now addressed the school; and what a long address! All this while, my nervousness increased, especially when I could see Gruff making rude faces when the headmaster was not looking as if to say that if he was caned I would answer for it. All eyes were fixed upon me and in my apprehension, I was sure that some of the pupils wondered whether I was a new thief caught red-handed in the headmaster's house or whether I was a small, humble but intellectual phenomenon of great consequence come to teach in this school.

What agony! I fidgeted, I stood to attention, I passed my right foot over the left one, itches bubbled up from I don't know where, but I dare not scratch, torrents of mucus threatened to course down to my nether lip but I dared not sniff, and dared not blow my nose—oh agony of agonies: I had no handkerchief! My body seemed to be playing a thousand sadistic games designed to disgrace me outright! Now my stomach growled as loudly as our dog had growled before my father taught it eternal silence—and I thought all the three hundred pairs of eyes turned upon me to condemn me for spoiling this solemn parade. Through the corner of my eye, I saw the School Captain leer at me, and I tried in vain to compress my stomach muscles from which I imagined that disgraceful growl had emanated. The growl was

28

repeated, louder this time and I heard some of the smaller boys of Standard Five blurt out in laughter. I was ashamed and embarrassed but still the head-master droned on. Inside, my stomach changed the tactics of disgrace. My bowels seemed to come flying apart and I could not control the rumbles that rolled on in rapid successions like bomb explosions utterly bewildering the headmaster out of authority—for I saw him roll his eyes towards me and *laugh*! Upon which the whole school took the cue and laughed too at my expense! For my part I did not laugh, but made myself look a great moron by rolling my eyes as if I was seeing ghosts.

When the laughter had died down somewhat, the headmaster addressed the school about me—causing further laughter, and when that had died down he began introducing me with the general observation that Kyambe Primary observed discipline within and without, that any student of *this* school knew better than to gorge himself into constipation and that he had sincere hopes that I would learn to adjust in time as I came from a 'backward' school. This adjective earned me the title 'Bushman' throughout that year.

Introduction over, the Standard Six prefect was called to take charge of me, and as I joined the class where I was to belong that year, the whole school clapped uproariously. But I noticed that the boy who had earlier challenged me to a fight (and who belonged to Standard Five) took advantage of this moment and shook his fist at me as a sure warning that soon he and I must fight whether I was constipated or not.

The parade was over and we were to work on the grounds the whole day. I have never had as long a day, as that twenty-third of January; have never been as mocked and tossed and ruffled and sneered at as

29

that twenty-third of January, have never scored so perfect a victory over a young Standard Five challenger in a fair fight, have never been admired for my fighting skill and thus made as many friends in the upper school as that twenty-third of January. And no figure ever presented itself before Hamad with as much pride and show and pomp when school was over, as I did on that twenty-third of January.

But Hamad was not happy and, contrary to my expectations, he did not congratulate me. Instead he gave me my food and watched me eat it in silence with a very thoughtful expression all over his face. At length he said, 'Kituku, people who fight end up badly.' After this he took his hoe and shovel and went down to the garden, where I soon heard the rhythmic thud of the hoe upon the ground.

'People who fight end up badly!'

Those words kept repeating themselves over and over within my mind and the more I heard them the more I was convinced that Hamad was wrong. Hadn't I felt the thrill of conquest? Hadn't I seen that young upstart spit two teeth on to the floor? And hadn't I been serenaded by the biggest boys in Standard Eight? Hadn't they shielded and spoken up for me when the School Captain had threatened to take me to the Master on Duty for correction? No; Hamad you are wrong! The winner is always right! The winner wins admiration, makes friends, is serenaded. How then can he end up badly? And with this conviction, I followed Hamad, determined to win him over.

He did not notice my presence but dug on. And I stood there admiring his bare, broad and muscular shoulders as he dug, whistling contentedly as he worked. I watched the soil heap up behind him and saw the brown dust waft into the wind with each blow of the hoe. He worked on, as if nothing could tire him, until he came to the end of the trench he was making. And now he became aware of me, greeted me genially and asked me whether the Young Scholar would like to develop his muscles with a few shovelfuls of soil. I agreed to this and jumped into the trench. Here was no father to supervise me. I used that shovel with great energy and enjoyment which positively affected Hamad and filled him with admiration for his little scholar friend, though I was very clumsy in the exercise. In this way we worked on, till the moon came up and all was quiet around us, except for the occasional burst of laughter from the builders. Shouldering our tools, we went to the pool in the brook and washed in the warm water. Now I felt I had demonstrated enough activity to press my point home about the fighter ending up well. But when I asked Hamad how it was that a fighter ended up badly he looked at me and, with his eyes shining, said that I was too young to know and that I should trust him when he advised me against fighting because he *knew*. The matter was closed for another few months when events forced me to ask him again.

Three

The days that followed saw me settling down both in school and at my new home—with various degrees of success. At school I made few friends among boys of my own age-group and particularly those of my class. I was long in discovering the reason for this hostility towards me until one Friday afternoon at parade, one

31

boy found it necessary to tread upon my toes to distract me from the headmaster's address. This caused me to cry out in as loud a voice as I could, causing all eyes to revolve towards me. Now the little rogue, who had been author of this mischief, was standing to attention, stiff as any pole upon earth, and listening to the headmaster with great concentration. Thus, upon the headmaster's asking who had made that noise, and upon my reply that 'We did it, sir!' little Joseph Matui (for this was the boy's name) stoutly denied it and began to cry to prove it. The upshot of this was that I was charged with double offence: of disturbing an orderly school parade, and of consciously trying to put another person into trouble. I was therefore to remain behind, take myself into the house of Correction, and await further developments.

When parade was over, I was going towards the house of penitence I referred to when little Joseph overtook me and, laughing straight into my face, he said, 'Don't think that just because you come top of the class at every weekly test you are cleverer than me. Some people are clever in more ways than one.'

I dashed after him but he was so fast and so nimble with his little feet that he made me trip and fall, and I cut a very stupid figure indeed.

Despite my indignation and anger, I could not help thinking with some degree of amusement how possible it was that such a wee insect as Matui could multiply himself to merit the title 'some people'. And as I entered the house of Correction, I was still toying with the thought that the legion that Christ had broken free from the pigs had found a better abode in little Joseph Matui.

I shall not dwell upon the terrors of the correction

house. Suffice it to say that when I walked out of the door and into freedom, I was not the same boy as had entered through it. There were tears rolling freely down my cheeks and I was wailing loudly, so that the boys who had been detained to work on the school-compound for not shutting their eyes during morning prayers—yes these little ones who were later to become criminals and end up in the hangman's noose for robbery with violence, looked at me and then bit their lips. I felt ashamed, not because the tears rolled down my cheeks (for those were a common sight in this school) but because the person who had punished me had been a woman—the same one who taught us religious studies. She had made me strip against my will. Upon which she had caned me, all the while commenting upon the nakedness and tormenting me by saying that she was sure that as I was an African boy who was no doubt the star of my village on account of my education, I must have a little wife stacked away somewhere. Then she had scrutinised my body as I put on my meagre pants and . . . laughed. I had not grown to like religious studies as *she* taught the subject. But now I was fully convinced that henceforth, I would never find it easy to like it, or to attend classes, let alone absorb the subject. For how could I bring myself to sit down in class before her without the knowledge that every time she looked at me she was laughing at me? She would not laugh scornfully about some irreligious, impious thing about African boys, as she had always done, without my feeling that I was the sole subject of the derision. How was I to endure her classes without the feeling that I was a lowly, common, shameful thing?

As I sit and reflect upon these days, now so far flushed along the river of history, I see before me

Kyambe School as it was then. Everything seemed to revolve around the subject of punishment. Let a pupil come late because he had been tending his mother in her illness, or because he had to wait for the river's flood to abate before he crossed it—he would be sermonised about education coming before everything else and end up black-listed for—punishment. Let him fail to knight the headmaster and the monosyllable 'sir' would be drummed into him in thorough punishment. Let the third and smallest daughter of Reverend Wranglem happen to wander into a classroom and the pupils therein fail to stand in her honour, the whole class would meet that well-fed monster: punishment. Let Wranglem be humorous in his sermons at the Chapel and let a boy laugh, the same would have punishment rattled about his ears. Let there be laughter in class, let there be woe, let there be stories, let there be play, let there be spectators of any game upon the grounds of Kyambe Primary and punishment would find a thousand ways to creep into all our activities in the person of one of his innumerable messengers. To a pupil, punishment was the first diet we had upon our first birthday into Kyambe academic life, and punishment was the staple diet upon which we were weaned. Punishment was the most memorable escort of every pupil that sighed with relief as he walked off Kyambe grounds, now a thoroughly flayed and harassed graduate, vowing never to set eyes upon this institution again.

I hated Kyambe School, and as I look back into the classrooms I went through, I see my classmates in various degrees of hatred of this school: some falling asleep and nodding upon their exercise books and pretending that they were only nodding agreement with what the moving oracle before us was either pronouncing or writing upon the black-board. I see some of them prop their heads with the palms of their hands, like so many bereaved children who must make the best of themselves to brave the hazards of life, now that no father or mother would ever take those little hands and lead the bearers through the darkness and into safety. I see us sitting in resignation; I see many of us stand up against the back wall with our hands stretched upright above our heads for as long as this class lasts. I see mouths open, and hear short covert bursts of laughter. And then the brief gleam of those children's teeth are no more. For the figure of Authority glares scorching fire at us. Always, always the teachers' monotonous voices drone on above our heads. I sit here and I hear the orders, 'write it down in your prep books'; 'the word is *and*, not "end", you little monkey! Say *and! and! and! aand!* Yes! Now write *that* pronunciation in your prep book a hundred times and let me have it before parade-time this evening.' The whack—whack of the cane always punctuates the air . . . A boy has just jumped through the window in mortal fear and I am sure I'll never see him again.

We are now in our English lesson and are all bending over our exercise books filling in the blanks—we are always filling in the blanks. To most of us, the whole exercise is ridiculous guesswork. The new teacher doesn't seem to know what he is about. That's why the blanks are so many. He won't explain anything, he won't lead us to discover anything. He just comes into class with 'blanks' written all over his face. I cannot see the difference between 'then' and 'when' and I am filling the blanks in a most unusual way: I have *then* and *when* written up on two pieces of paper, which are rolled into tight balls, and the whole exercise is performed the way our current politicians go about their secret ballots: I juggle the two paper balls in my hands, smell them, dance them under the desk to confuse the whole issue of identity, pick one up, unroll it and fill in a blank. I have filled in number eight in the list and it reads, 'I shall go home *then* the school is closed', and I get punished for this mistake.

English lesson! English lesson and blanks and interminable pronunciations of guttural sounds, of lisping sounds, of nasal sounds and *ba-ba* sounds and *baa* sounds and *um*-sounds, in which the forty-five of us make blabbering idiots of ourselves, and the whole classroom is a perfect bedlam. English lessons and vocabulary; the same procedure day in day out: 'Take out your dictionaries' and *whup*! Flash comes green Dic (as we christened that Authority), who says on his front cover that he is a very concise dictionary and gives a formidable impression of guarding most jealously, what lies thereafter: 'Take out your dictionaries—and study the words on page . . .' I *am* studying the words on page . . . but they don't mean anything to me. There's a word called 'gargoyle'— which sounds rather funny. We make no attempt to *learn the words nor even define t*hem. They come from the dictionary into our heads and evaporate with the evening air at the end of the lesson. We are told to write a composition about any of the words we have been studying. I like this word 'gargoyle'. I couldn't make head or tail of the definition. But it *must* be a good word, or the teacher would not have chosen the page that bore it. I seek to uplift the word and define it in terms of the invincible mortals of this school that I dread most, in order to please them, using *gargoyle* as an adjective of praise. Thus my composition reads, 'Our English teacher is very gargoyle, the headmaster is very gargoyle, and we have a school motto that says English should be spoken even in our dreams instead of our vernacular and, God's truth! that's very gargoyle!—the Chapel is gargoyle, Reverend Wranglem is gargoyle, punishment and school rules are very gargoyle because they make us grow to be good boys when we leave Kyambe School, which I think is altogether very gargoyle indeed . . .'

I end my composition with a self-satisfied parenthesis that I hope my teacher has found my work to be a very gargoyle composition and that he might be motivated to give me a gargoyle present.

It is parade time and the list of offenders is being read. My name is first on the list and the charges are numerous—disrespect for my seniors, big-headedness, hatred of my school, irreligious conduct and questioning of School Motto et-cetera. I am to be punished in full view of the school, for misuse of consecrated gargoyle.

Then there is a monstrous sounding subject called Rural Science. I don't have a clue what 'Rural' means, but I think it does for all purposes on this earth. But I like the word 'Science' and so I look forward to the subject with glowing enthusiasm. There is a map of England with a crown at the top of it, though I don't know what particular island the crown is supposed to represent. But the teacher is busy explaining something about Rural Science in England. It is the end of the lesson and he is testing our understanding in the last twenty minutes. Upon his pointing at a picture on the map, and asking what that particular object is, the whole class roars in chorus—which cacophony our teacher seems to enjoy. Thus we sing that what's denoted is 'Rural sheep'; 'Rural Zoo', 'Rural city',

'Rural cows', 'Rural fish', 'Rural sea . . .''And that?' asks the teacher, pointing at the crown: 'Rural crown,' we chorus.

'Good!' says he, 'the lesson is over!' We are very happy. He told us 'Good!' We all like Rural Science. It sounds very intelligent and it encompasses everything. We wonder why this teacher is not allowed to be our sole instructor for everything. It would be so easy and much in tune with our intellectual aspirations. We would have Rural Mathematics, Rural English, Rural Bible Study, Rural Civics, History and Geography. Everything would be simply Rural. But the White District Education Officer doesn't like our teacher. I see the former coming into our class one hot afternoon and sitting at the back of the class. Our teacher is trembling. And most of us are looking at the visitor. Our teacher wants to make the visitor one of us and he tells me, 'Kituku!'

'Sir.'

'Welcome our visitor in the manner of this school.'

'Yes, sir.'

I stand up, get out of my desk, stand to an enviable military attention and, looking at the general direction of the D.E.O. and about five metres above him— (we are never allowed to look anyone in the face for that is bad manners), I say, 'Welcome to our visitor,' in the distinguished manner of Kyambe School, 'Welcome, sir. Be one of us, sir. We are going to learn Rural Science in England, sir.'

Wonder of wonders! the visitor smiles on me and claps. He says, 'Thank you.' We all clap, including myself.

Our teacher is highly encouraged and emboldened. He decides to take that boldness a step further and involve our distinguished guest a little more. He is saying that the visitor is a Rural D.E.O. in Rural Kenya Colony, that he is a Rural Englishman under a Rural Sovereign, and he came here by Rural ship . . . The D.E.O. is red with rage. He is holding our teacher by the scruff of his neck and shouting, 'Get out! Get out you bloody stupid oaf.'

The following day our teacher is not with us. At morning parade, the headmaster says that our teacher was found guilty of 'fraud' and 'impersonation' (these words baffled me till I got into high school). He adds that from then henceforth, Standard Six Rural Science will be taken by himself. Our faces fall. Henceforth Rural Science would be nothing but roaring and caning . . .

From then on, I hated school more and more and had I not a good sing-song memory which always placed me first or second position in class, I would have been miserable indeed. Indeed my life in Kyambe School would have been utterly miserable, especially in my first term if Hamad had not always been there to counterbalance it. I see him pass before my eyes so many, many times. I see the hoe flash and glitter in the low sun of many evenings; I see the dust rise in the garden. I see this garden take shape, get cleaner and cleaner in readiness for planting. And always there is this lone man, all his concentration bent upon his work, his broad shoulders and heavy chest never tiring, but working, working and working.

Out of the gloom of school and evening, and walking dejectedly towards the hut, I see a small boy, clad in khaki uniform, with a bulging school bag slung over his shoulder. I see the boy arrive home. And on seeing the boy, the servant leaves his work and walks up to the hut. They meet and greet, cordially, like a man and his younger brother. Now the younger brother is feeding. There is always food in this house. And the elder is standing watching, smiling at his handiwork—for the younger boy grows fat with each passing day. I see the boy wandering out to the brook or venturing to the outskirts of the forest—and always the older man stands under the eaves, always watching over the boy. He too is very glad, as if the thrill the boy feels at the touch of the green eucalyptus leaves or that of the rippling brook which has considerably subsided because of the drought, or the thrill that fills the boy's heart at the murmurs and whispers of the leaves in the wind—all this thrill, he also feels.

It is evening, and the boy is reading or doing homework. As I waft closer and peer over his exercise book, I see he's doing something he calls 'prep', but the title is 'arithmetic'. There is a sentence here: 'If 236 fruits in 4 boxes weigh 203 kilograms, and if 1 fruit weights 0.33 kilograms, calculate the weight of each box.'

At first he's mesmerised by it all, but he struggles on until he arrives at an answer. The elder brother pores over the problem as if he understands it. And when the boy beams with pleasure at the solution to his problem, the man also smiles with satisfaction, as if the problem has been *his* also, and he had helped in solving it. The latter sits thoughtfully, pondering over the magic of letters and words. On many an evening, when the boy is poring over his books, when it is quiet and no sound penetrates the dark silence that shrouds the land, and the hyena, the jackal, and fox— yes—even the cicada—have all gone to sleep and nothing stirs except the pages of the boy's book, I see him, always looking at the boy with something akin to wonder both over his face and in his keen bright eyes. Then I hear him say, 'My young brother, teach me how to read and write.'

The boy is taken aback by this request and I hear him say, 'But you are old! You cannot go back to Standard One. Where shall I begin, when you are so old?'

The man is stung. I see his face before me and it tells me that he *knows* he is old, but also that he must know this magic of words and figures.

At length he says, 'Yes I *am* old. But I *will* learn. I shall begin where you began. Let's begin there.'

It is agreed. And for many hours, they struggle through the practice for loosening the hand. Innumerable a's, b's, and c's are written singly, then joined. One exercise book is full and then they are on the second one. Now the man is writing out all the alphabet and his hand is firm and round. Both beam at the progress. Next they are working on the combination of letters—the writing of names, of sentences, of paragraphs . . . The numbers have not been left out, I see them adding two and two on the exercise book. And I hear the laughter of both of them. But, above all, I hear the perpetual melody of the guitar that slices across the layers of these many intervening years and arrives to resound, within my ears, pure and unblemished. I see the boy sitting before the guitar and its player,—three silhouettes outlined against the dying embers—for it is very late in the night. Long after the last spark died and it is dark, I still hear the melody and the words of the song, interspersed with the soft snores of the boy. The man has poked the fire, for the embers are alive again. And he gathers up the snoring boy into his arms, places him on the bed and covers him. Then he returns to the guitar and strums again. He breaks the song in mid-stanza and stretches forth his hand for his books and pencil. And I see him labour deep into the night, murmuring to himself, 'I must know. I *must know*.'

The days roll on. I see the boy now holding that guitar. He is still all thumbs and laboriously plays note by note with a single finger. Gradually I see him move his fingers at different places along the strings. And the man is always there, encouraging. This evening the boy is playing the song whose words he does not know. And his eyes are shut tight as if he too were part of the story of the song.

'Hamad?'

'Mmh?'

'The song . . .'

'What about it?'

'What does it mean?'

'It is personal. I made it up myself. I'd rather not tell you.'

'No. You must tell me. You promised . . .'

'All right. Tomorrow, when, you come back from school. Now you are tired. Go to bed, young teacher. Go to bed. It is very late.'

'But . . .'

'I said, "Go to bed!" '

* * *

It was the first time I had seen Hamad in such fury. Yet it was not fury only. There was a sort of urgency, of fear—as if he was in court and being tortured to tell a secret, which to divulge would earn him a sure death. There was nothing for me to do but to go to bed. Although I shut my eyes I could still see him through my eye-lashes as he sat before the fire, sad and mute. And he sat thus until the fire went out. Long afterwards I heard him breathe heavily and rummage through the pile in the corner in search of his bedding. Then he stretched out on the floor and slept. As sleep overtook me, I thought about Hamad: brother, friend, sad, uneducated, yearning to learn.

The following day I learned little. It was one of those days when all the teachers seemed to be in murderous moods and when all their faces assumed uniformly ugly contortions as if they had all taken the cue from Reverend Wranglem's colossal bulldog. At morning parade, the headmaster reported that some bad behaviour was creeping into the school. The night before, some boys had been caught red-handed in the crime of attending a dance, and dancing like the pagans Reverend Wranglem had so laboriously and repeatedly warned us against. The headmaster then left the platform for Reverend Wranglem to tell us exactly why going to a 'bush dance' at night was unchristian and against the rules of morality. He began by absolving himself of all responsibility for the words he was about to utter. The words were holy, came straight from the hand of God and he was nothing more than an earthly mouthpiece. Then he opened his Bible and read as he had done every other Sunday at Chapel, that *we* were washed clean, that *we* should not be equally yoked with unbelievers and that *we* should flee from among them. He ended by emphasizing his sermon with, 'Thus saith the Lord,' while shutting his Bible with a snap as if to cut short all further possible argument upon that subject. After that he stormed out of the meeting and I caught a glimpse of him marching up the hillock towards the lone mansion that was his Kenyan house, with the attitude of one who had surely been thoroughly let down by the ungrateful wretches that we were.

Now the headmaster began to speak and, slowly

and deliberately, called out the list of offenders. And first, of a long list, was Gruff. (His real name was Kiamba-wa-Maundu.) The headmaster then directed that the offenders come forward into the square. Slowly the culprits filtered out of the ranks and huddled together in the middle of the square—a sad woebegone little bunch of young people. Once I had seen chickens caught in the heavy long rains of April. I had seen these drooping wet chickens huddle together on the verandah because no one would open the door for them. And I had heard their plaintive cackle to comfort one another as they huddled yet more closely together. Looking at these boys assembled before us reminded me of those chickens, and the sadness I had felt so long before now came afresh.

They stood there, close, tightly packed, all fidgeting, rubbing their cracked feet, wet with the morning dew, upon one another. And all stared at the ground, feeling the condemnation of the whole upright school upon them, listening to the headmaster.

His voice came upon us all like the seventh angel's voice on judgement day: that the miserable lot before us was the seed of the Evil One; that they were a shame to the school, to their parents, to their community and to their God; that no punishment was fit for these misfits and that he must be given time to meditate. Then he called all the staff and the School Captain to his office to confer. And we stood there, waiting.

It must have been an hour before they re-appeared. And now the headmaster spoke about those that were bowed down before us.

'Do you all see the result of evil?' said he, pointing at the group. 'They dare not look at us, for they know they have done wrong. Look up!'

44

Slowly the faces came up, one by one. But they could not meet the glare of six hundred eyes, particularly those of the senior authorities of the school. The faces of guilt looked up at the sky as if expecting a solace there but one that wouldn't come. They looked at the mountains, at rooftops, at the ground before our feet, at everything visible upon the grounds and surroundings of Kyambe Primary . . . but never at us. For endless minutes, the headmaster said nothing. The school said nothing. No sound relieved the tension. We all stood there mute, at attention, gazing at those offenders.

There was among them a small boy of about my own size and age. As the silence intensified, I heard him sob once and then wail outright. And then the whole school let out a sigh of relief—and a shuffling of feet because in that heavy condemning silence, a human voice had been heard. At last the headmaster cleared his throat and announced the verdict. He began by affirming the age-old true proverbs that, 'A thorny tree germinates with its thorns intact,' and that, 'No leopard-cub will sport spots without the mother leopard having them.' The upshot of this ancestoral wisdom was that the offenders should go home and come with their parents in the afternoon of the same day.

It was at this time that the headmaster noted that Gruff had not come out for identification and he called out: 'Maundu!' For his part, Gruff was standing at the corner of his classroom building and, partly hidden by the front row of Standard Eight, he was coolly chewing gum as if the whole exercise was ridiculous and so much insignificant bother.

'Maundu!' the headmaster repeated.

Maundu raised his eyebrows.

'Maundu, come out here!'

Maundu came out and, hands in his pockets, he swaggered to the group of offenders, surveyed them with utmost scorn, and stood with arms akimbo, rudely chewing his gum and glaring at the headmaster.

'Take those hands out of your pockets and learn manners!' the headmaster barked. But his voice was now high and whiny. Gruff smiled and I could see his tongue rolling the chewing gum nonchalantly inside his mouth.

'*You* come and take them out. I like them where they are.'

For a long time, no one spoke. At last I heard the air whistle from the headmaster's throat and he said, 'This must get to your father!'

Then Gruff moved, slouching towards the headmaster who backed, and seemed to grow smaller as the towering giant drew nearer and nearer.

He stopped right in front of the headmaster and, arms still akimbo, Gruff said, 'You go and tell my father. I have done nothing wrong. I was at school on time, what does it matter to *you* what I did last night?'

With that Gruff walked back into his classroom, emerged with his school bag and got on to his motorcycle which was propped behind the classroom. The last I heard of him that day was his horn blaring incessantly, as if announcing Doomsday. Behind him, the headmaster came down upon us with fury and vigour and he talked lengthily about discipline and school rules. We were not to learn that day. The whole school was to work on the grounds to strengthen those walls of discipline crumbling down with us.

All through that day, we looked forward to the

evening with feelings akin to horror. Throughout the day, we speculated on what the headmaster would do to the culprits after he had met their parents. Time passed slowly, very slowly, defying the wishes of the young minds for him to hurry up and get it over with. We worked on, under the merciless prefects who were generally the stupidest pupils in the whole school but who were the most adept at brutality and discipline.

The bell rang and, laying down our tools, we hurried to parade. The headmaster was there long before us, surveying his boys as we dashed to take our places. As in the morning, the culprits were huddled together at the centre of the courtyard. And as in the morning, they looked at everything but us. Nothing had changed: the same sombre air, made even more threatening by the dark clouds assembled on all horizons, the same tortured offenders, the same obedient school boys, standing at an attention posture any hardened disciplinarian would have been proud of; the same dark-faced staff upon whose faces the name of discipline was hallowed—the same little headmaster, belligerent as ever, disciplined and disciplining as ever, moralistic as ever and knowing more than anyone present how children *must* behave.

Nothing was changed, I say, except the group of bewildered parents of the offenders. These parents were grouped together at the other end of the courtyard (opposite the headmaster) and talking in low voices. They were a sad collection of people, and, as we went home, I knew that every boy felt the same indignation at seeing these parents wrenched from their duties to attend school. Many of them could not even boast of a decent piece of clothing, which consisted of either shirts and trousers or dresses whose original colours were long faded and overlaid with a light dirt-brown colour that was the result of repeated washing. As for those pieces of cloth, the mender had been so busy upon them that it was difficult to tell what the original cloth had been, having been patched up with any available piece, regardless of colour, from top to bottom. There were two very old men there, with blankets draped across their shoulders, who leaned on their long staffs, looking tired and worn out and I wondered when they would ever get to their homes . . . for the sun was rapidly descending towards the western mountains.

The headmaster cleared his throat and began: that it was a great honour for those esteemed parents to entrust him with their children; that because their children were in school most of the time, it was his socially and God-given duty to be second-parent to them, that in this duty he was assisted by specially trained, God-fearing people, 'as you see assembled before you' (this with a flourish of hands to enfold all the teachers of Kyambe).

Thus the school was as one family. Now, for a home and a family to keep together, it was necessary to have some rules by which to live, just as there must be rules to keep *your* families together. Wasn't that so Mzee Kitua? Mzee Kitua, the oldest of the parents present, murmured that he believed it was so.

'Good,' said the headmaster, highly encouraged by the old man. He then enlarged upon the school rules: there were rules moral, rules religious, rules social, rules economic, rules political, rules historically African versus rules historically English, by which these two mortal species were to be kept asunder as sunset did sunrise; for it *was* decreed in the days of Noah that the offspring of Good Japheth shall forever be lords, and for ever enslave the evil descendants of

48

mannerless Ham whose·sons and daughters we were. Rules! Rules!—the headmaster explained them all and qualified their infliction on us with the fact they were for our own good. And the parents stood there, mute, unable to comprehend all this rigmarole. From where I stood, I saw the face of Reverend Wranglem, looking at this group over his garden hedge and his face seemed to glow, as if the parent's failure to know anything about these rules was divine confirmation of the wide unbridgeable gap between them and him. In that glow was the kind of paternalism which I detested and which had so nettled me every Sunday when the pastor of my father's local Church had patted my head for reading the text of his choice for the day's sermon.

The headmaster went on: that there was a rule against exposure of your young children to pagan dances, for then they would get spoilt. In your time Mzee Kitua, did young children the age of these go to dances?—Mzee Kitua seemed to come out of a reverie into which the yardage of rules had thrown him, and mumbled something midway between yes and no. The headmaster bypassed Mzee Kitua and continued with great conviction that these boys had contravened *that* law, and were to be punished. But since the headmaster did not know what kind of punishment to hand out for such an offence which endangered the future of a whole location, 'tribe' and colony, he had thought it wise to ask the parents to handle that responsibility, for *they* were these offenders' flesh and blood.

At a gesture from the headmaster, the school captain produced a bundle of well-polished canes. Then our headmaster described the system of punishment. As the name of each offender was called, the

49

parent concerned would march forward, select a cane and punish his or her son in full view of the school.

The show began.

The first hand of punishment was a mother; the son got punishment enough to make him cry, upon which she stopped, threw the stick aside, and went back to her group. Everyone followed the same procedure: a parent came forward, beat the child, the child cried, the parent threw away the stick, and went back. But as the exercise continued, I noticed that the boys who had been caned first would laugh at the one currently under punishment. I was at a loss to understand how anyone would laugh under such circumstances until an accident occurred to change the course of events: a thoroughly belligerent man was caning his son with more vigour than had been shown that day, and the loud whack of the cane was heard far beyond the confines of the school compound. Yet the boy did not wince, not even once, and I was setting him up as an example of endurance when I noticed an unusual object protruding below his pants. The harder the parent hit, the faster this thing slid until, tired of all this assault, it dropped to the floor with a clatter that only an angel and hardened buffalo hide could produce. Down came the cane with the usual vigour and this time the boy yowled and jumped up! At which the whole school came down with laughter. Even the *headmaster* laughed.

When peace was restored, the headmaster became stern again and said that *the parents were joking* and that the remaining boys would be caned by himself. The seven were made to bend: then the headmaster tapped them to see whether there was anything foreign to school uniform guarding their buttocks, at the end of which exercise many 'foreigners' lay at the feet of each boy in a resigned penitent attitude as if to say, 'Sorry I let you down.' Only one boy hadn't worn a 'stranger' between his uniform and his buttocks. This was the boy who had cried in the morning, and now he stood with haunted horror spread all over his face.

The laughter that greeted the headmaster's discovery was tremendous. Out front, Reverend Wranglem who had now returned to witness these events was doubled with laughter, the School Captain was convulsed, the sober faces of the staff displayed sets of beautiful teeth and the whole parade shook like ripe corn in the wind. In all my stay at Kyambe School, I never saw the school parade as merry as it was at that moment. All were having the time of their lives except the parents who didn't think it was funny at all, and the seven who were about to go through the ordeal.

At length the laughter died down and the headmaster began. And I saw the school wince with each stroke and heard the voice of the sufferer cry out with it. Then it was quiet. Out of the silent group of parents an old man limped forward. Slowly, he approached the scene of punishment and took by the hand, the little boy that had cried in the morning.

'You shall not beat my son!' he said, trembling all over. 'You will not beat my last born. I gave all my sons to the likes of him (pointing at Reverend Wranglem) to fight their wars—I was told they would come back the greatest warriors in this land. Instead only a word came back to me: and the word was death. Instead I got this—(said he, producing a cloth medal ribbon of many colours). I got *this* and the thanks of your King. What is *this* to my sons?' he asked us all, throwing the medal on the floor. 'Now you want to take my last born the same way and I will not allow it.'

The headmaster retorted, raising his voice authoritatively, 'Old man, go back to the others. This boy must be punished. There are school-rules to be kept . . . .'

'School rules, your mother's anus! What *are* school rules which produce tears? In all my family life I have always had rules. And not once did my children cry out—And they have been honest, dutiful and happy. This boy here has never lied to me, has never done a wrong thing without owning up to it, without our discussing it, without my forgiving him. And that wrong has never been repeated. This boy here has never cried of punishment from *my* hand. Ever since I brought him here he has always come home to me in tears. What new rules are these that don't bring happiness?'

'Old man, I'm telling you . . .,' began the headmaster.

'Shut up you!' roared the old man, striking him. 'Have you ever known the pain of bringing up children, eh? A little boy of yesterday who thinks his head touches the heavens! Have you no shame, bandying words with me?'

The old man spat and, taking his son by the hand, limped slowly off the school compound, with the headmaster's harangue about the Government taking up the matter falling on his unheeding ears. And the headmaster was true to his word. A year later, the old man was picked from his hut by the askari and locked up for being anti-government by not paying his hut tax. He later died in prison a few months after that—an old, lonely, man whom nobody dared to visit for fear of being marked down and victimized.

When the old man had left, the whole school assumed an eerie silence broken only by the smack—whack—smack of the cane, and the cries of the six boys. Gruff was not present, and the headmaster prudently steered off this subject. I was not surprised therefore, when Gruff turned up the next day and, having spent an hour in the headmaster's office, was punished by having to collect pieces of paper around the classrooms. Thereafter he was absolved of all evil and was allowed to go back to class.

It was nearing sunset when I arrived home. The clouds were still gathering, and as I passed across the fields I noticed that all the cows were looking up into the air and sniffing at it. Then they would bellow and, twisting their tails, they would jump up in the air and stampede round the pastures, bellowing with joy. As I walked home I thought about parade and the old man, and wondered why we were so fond of pain, why we were always initiated and educated into pain and what had happened to the laughter I had always felt as I tended animals such as these—simple beasts that were not *afraid* to show their joy? Once my father had told me that I was far more superior to these cows because God had given me a mind. What use was that mind if it forbade the experience of joy and happiness? I thought about this as I walked on home, towards Hamad and his mysterious story.

Four

I found him beside the grass-thatched house. Like the cows, he was looking up at the clouds. A smile was spread over his face, making it look smooth and as open and innocent as a baby's. He was so absorbed by the darkening sky that he did not immediately become aware of my presence, and I was obliged to follow his example and look up. The east was one dark wall of cloud that seemed to rise from the depths of the earth behind the hills. The setting sun shone upon the silvery tops of the cloud above us, giving it the appearance of an immense arching rainbow. It was an awesome sight, made even more so by the slight-wind which was rising, carrying with it the odour of moist earth.

Presently, Hamad became aware of me and stifled an exclamation, as if he had been communing secretly with someone up in the clouds and was ashamed of being found out.

'It'll rain tonight,' I said, to break the silence.

'Yes, and heavily too.'

He was silent for a while. I took my bag inside and came out again. Then as if there was no subject other than the sky, Hamad said abruptly:

'I think it will be a storm!'

'What?'

'The rain. It will be a storm. I saw the sky like this only once before and the storm that followed was deadly!'

I was silent, not knowing what to say to that. Up

above, the cloud ate up the last rays of sunlight and the earth was half-swallowed in a dark and gloomy twilight. We went into the hut to prepare dinner. Presently I came out with a bucket and went to the brook to fetch water. The wind was gathering and it was getting darker. The excited voices of the builders reached me as I hoisted the bucket on to my head and I hurried to find out what they were excited about.

Hamad and the seven of them were assembled before the big house and all were looking at the direction of the school. I put the bucket inside and joined them on the verandah. The sight made my heart thump faster. Above the school the cloud was giving way and a dark leg of rain was slowly pouring down towards earth. The deep hum of the pouring water was clearly audible from where we stood. Then it touched down, and both the school and the hillock on which it was built were lost to us. A zigzag blade of lightning ran twice upwards from earth to sky. Then the thunder rumbled across the whole sky and, as if that was a signal to open the heavens, the roar of water filled the sky with a deafening sound. Then the hail began to fall, in large pebbles which hit the earth with immense fury. Hamad and I dived into the hut. The storm had begun.

The rain came down in thick sheets, driven at great speed and fury by the wind. Soon there was a continuous roar as the brook near the house began to swell. Everything was swallowed in the roaring storm and the thunder that rumbled incessantly, followed by a harsher onslaught of still more rain. Our roof was leaking. At first, big drops hit the centre of the floor, followed by other drops all over the house. We rolled the bedding to one side of the bed and stacked everything under it. Over in the corner the guitar strings glittered against the fire and as I looked at the guitar, I was reminded of a baby sleeping peacefully, unmindful of the terrors raging outside.

The storm raged on. It raged through our preparation for dinner, and our eating it, the putting away of dishes, and the constant poking of the fire and feeding it more dry sticks lest the leaking water put it out.

How long we sat, listening to the roar all around us, I cannot say. But all the wood Hamad had gathered was now gone, and the fire was in danger of going out as the leaking roof grew weaker and let in more rain. And still the storm raged on, fiercer than ever before.

At length I began to doze, and in these moments of intermittent sleep I never lost the consciousness that outside that storm was raging. By and by, Hamad shifted the bed to a safer area and unrolled the bedding upon which I tossed myself and fell into deep sleep. This time I dreamt. And in my dream an earthen guitar formed itself out of the storm, developed legs and kept playing a song I knew I had always wanted to sing but could not. If I could get hold of that guitar, I would know the mystery of the song. Thus I stretched out my hand to grab it. But the harder I stretched out, the further into the turbulent sky the guitar receded—the song growing fainter and more precious. And out of the stormy sky, out of the bowels of the guitar someone was speaking, 'I am everything. If the body were not this body, then I am everything. Awake therefore and say—I am everything . . .'

'Awake! Awake! Awake!'

I woke up with a start, trying hard to hold the vanishing message.

56

'Wake up!' the voice repeated. I nearly jumped up in terror. But the iron hand that had shaken my shoulder, now held me down. Then I came back to earth and was relieved to find that only Hamad was there, a sure safeguard against the terrible storm and darkness, which I was mortally afraid of.

'What is it?' I cried.

'Sh . . . listen!'

I sat up.

At first I heard nothing save the roaring storm. Then, out of the turbulence, a human voice faintly reached us. Hamad opened the door and went outside, letting in a strong blast of wind that set aglow the dying embers. I followed him. Before us, the mist and rain enveloped everything so that the nearest tree appeared a very ghost. The sound came nearer, more distinct this time. Then there was a lull of the roaring wind and the sound was unmistakable: the agonised wail of a small child. And it was coming from the direction of the river.

'Light the fire,' Hamad said, urgently.

'Now? What shall I . . . ?'

'Use anything but light that fire—*Now*,' he rasped. 'I'll be back soon.'

And, grabbing a hoe-handle, he plunged into the turmoil.

Left behind, I was both afraid and bewildered and, despite my strict Christian upbringing in which the spirits of the dead were nothing but the twin efforts of both the Devil and Imagination, I could not silence the thumping dread within me that kept saying the voice out there was a ghost, and that Hamad had surely been called by this being; that he would not come back and I was alone in this hut—in this night of ghosts and moaning wind. My first impulse was to wake the builders. But no! To get there I had to cross thirty metres of mist and wind and rain—and certainly the ghost lurked there—beneath the sighing and the moaning eucalyptus trees. I had to stay here, in the hut, and make a blaze, big enough to scare any ghost. I plunged into the corner of the hut. No wood! I plundered the other corner—and the guitar clanged and twanged, driving me almost out of my mind in terror. No wood! Outside, everything was wet. And I dare not venture out beyond the door. There was nothing to do but try the rafters, that formed the eaves. This I did. Soon a sizable bundle of wood, sisal and grass was heaped beside the hearth, illuminated by the blazing fire. And then I sat, waiting.

For long minutes I sat there, with the fear growing within me that any minute now, a ghost would burst through that door, put out the fire and maul me about. Then I remembered the guitar and, taking it into my arms like a dear child, I began to play. I played all the chords I had either learned or had invented on my own. I heaped some more wood and grass on to the fire that now had burned low, took the guitar again, and began to hum a song. I felt confident then—as if the music would stand a sure safeguard against any foe . . .

Suddenly the door burst open and they stood there, the ghosts I had dreaded. I yelped in terror and dived into the nearest corner, praying silently that if it be true I was to be devoured, then it were better it were done at once. When I dared look again, I noticed that they had all come into the hut—all the four of them—and that they were busy unloading themselves of the belongings they carried—which belongings were in a dripping, sorry state. Then I recognized them.

There was Hamad, cheerful and strong as ever. On

his right hip and protected by his strong left hand, sat a young boy of about four or five years. He had a rather large head, and in the firelight, his eyes seemed dull and popping out. I had a fleeting feeling and hope that he should not cough, lest they bolt out of his head altogether. Below this head, the chin darted out angrily and pointedly as if the owner had to develop that part either for constant warfare with fowls or for pecking at grains. Seen against Hamad's side, this boy seemed to be making a silent plea to change heads and I was at a great loss to know how such a child could have been reduced to so miserable a state.

Another was a woman, or the remains of what must have been a robust and good-looking woman. She was of medium height, with an abundance of hair that was carefully bundled and tightly packed beneath a white headdress. Like the child, the most obvious feature about her was a beautiful and rather protruding forehead, beneath which were a pair of eyes so brown and dull that it was a wonder she could see through them. Beneath them was a short small nose, whose nostrils kept dilating up and down as if she was perpetually sniffling. But this was compensated by a very pretty little mouth, but whose tightly arched lips gave me the impression that those lips did not communicate very often. She was rather strong-looking in other features, with strong arms and legs along which her veins traced their courses like a crisscross of paths upon a bare hillside. She wore a faded white dress which clung to her body, because of the rain, and made her bunch up, in an attempt to still the shivers that racked her body every few seconds.

And behind them, and stooping above the three as if to offer endless blessing, hovered the one man I had always dreaded meeting again. He seemed to have

59

acquired more clothing since we met last so many months before. Now he was bundled up in a long raincoat, beneath which his jacket and shirt seemed to burst through at the neck. This raincoat gave way to a yardage of scarf, wound several times around his neck so that his head stuck out of this mass of wool like a stark question mark crowning an insoluble problem. And, as on the day he stood beside my father, Kyanzo's questioning head hovered over everyone before him, as if they were a problem he couldn't solve, with the attitude of one given to advising the whole world that the problem was insoluble, was as old as time, that he had always known it and must never be bothered about it because he had passed his verdict upon it. He still had the same python eyes that surveyed me up and down, in the most quizzical manner; the same bloodthirsty lick of his lips as if the water trickling from his hair down to his upper lip was not enough but he must add to it the blood of all present.

My host now surveyed the whole room, decided that everything was all wrong and how on earth could we put a bed in *that* corner? Upon this revelation, Hamad and I jumped into action and placed the bed where *he* wanted it. Then he attacked the positioning of utensils: did any man, however stupid, ever dream of putting food *and* utensils under a *bed*? Hamad politely put in a word about saving them from the leaking roof, 'Master!'

'Leaking roof!' my host remonstrated, and then screamed. 'What's more important, you fool—leaking roof or hygiene?'

Hamad's face went blank at the prospect of making a survival choice between a leaking roof and all hygiene on earth. So we sorted out the flour packets from the bean packets, the maize packets from the potato packets and all these from both the bed and the utensils.

'Tend to the fire—*you*!'

The last monosyllable was flung to the whole room and denoted no one in particular; so no one did anything until my host, Kyanzo, straightened up, and arms akimbo, glared at his wife until she unfolded her hands and began to tend the fire.

Everything was changed under Kyanzo's supervision to such a degree that by the time he was satisfied, the whole house looked like an army barracks with the various battalions of household belongings standing to attention for his inspection. Only the guitar had not been assigned a place. It lay in the centre of the room, where I had left it. Kyanzo now saw it, and looked at it askance, like a dog that wanted a piece of meat but in which it smelt danger. Then with one shove of his long legs, he sent the guitar clattering along the floor to the farthest wall. I saw Hamad stand still, his eyes blazing as he looked at his master.

'Take that thing away from my sight and never let me see it again. For on the day I see it before me again, or even hear it, I will make firewood of it.'

Kyanzo said this in such a way and with such cold finality that even Hamad's anger seemed to melt into a limpid pool. Slowly he picked up the instrument and went out. Soon after, I heard him knocking at the main house, and when he returned, he did not have the guitar.

When our unpacking and re-arrangements were over, we sat down around the fire, and a silent miserable looking group we were. Up till now, no one had greeted anyone else or asked after the well-being of anyone, or even made introductions. We just sat, silent, as if talking required an enormous expenditure of all our faculties. At length, the head of the house decided to open communications and, turning towards me, asked how I fared at school. I was going into all the merits and demerits of Kyambe School when he cut me short and repeated the question, using the exact same words. I replied that I was doing both well and not so well.

'That's no answer!' he rasped. 'When your father asks me I'm not going to say you are doing well and not so well.' Upon which I corrected myself and said I was doing well. I was so harassed and prodded and turned about that, by the time I had finished with answering, I felt an abject liar and left Kyambe the fountain of all wisdom—worldly and spiritual. But my host didn't seem to be pleased and recommended that I should do better and never slack; that I must go to Church, obey my teachers and follow their instructions to the letter. He further recommended that at my age we (my school mates and I) should never be kept far from the cane; for the cane was a sure road to obedience. He turned to Hamad and asked him how I fared at this home, whether I was obedient, whether I worked in the garden after school, whether I cooked, whether I studied in the evenings—to all of which (and more), Hamad replied in my best interest so that any earthly father or guardian would proudly point and say, 'Behold my son, in whom I am well-pleased.'

But Kyanzo was *not* pleased. He *must* find fault with me. And this came in the person of Hamad and the guitar: that my host had caught me red-handed with that terrible instrument of evil, that he had listened awhile and he was convinced that I had been

62

playing 'that thing' for quite some time else I wouldn't be so adept at it. What did I say to that?

I had to admit involving myself with base pagan emotions under the influence of a base instrument. 'I might have to see your headmaster about that!'

My heart sank! My mind went racing back to the weeping boy and I wondered whether Kyanzo or my father would stand up to the headmaster and defend his love for me. I saw myself, alone in that courtyard, six hundred eyes upon me, my classmates (especially that little dog of a Matui) laughing at my expense. If that happened . . .! If that happened . . .! My mind wouldn't come to a resolution then, but I knew I would never stand that humiliation.

The voice of judgement now turned upon Hamad. But except for harbouring that pagan instrument for which accusation he got off lightly because *he* was pagan himself and was under no enlightened spiritual obligations, Hamad's performance all round seemed to please his master greatly, and he gave him more responsibility. Beginning 'tomorrow' he would extend the garden across the brook. He would begin by hewing the trees, that the principle may be glorified that to whom much is given, more shall be added. In this process I was to be Hamad's assistant, that I might learn the virtue of hard work, domestic discipline, and, obedience.

It was when ne turned upon the question of the builders that my host found grounds to vent all his simmering anger. When he heard that the house had not been completed because the money he had given was not enough to buy the necessary iron sheets, Kyanzo stood still and roundly castigated all those liars. No, they must have spent the money! They were a bunch of cretins who ought not to have been assigned this job, and he wondered what colossal idiot had hired them! Who did they think they were? Why did they work only nine hours a day, instead of twelve or thirteen? Why didn't they utilize the bright moonlight? No! He would reduce their salaries by half! My host would have continued this attack against the vice of laziness, had he not found that beast under his very nose. 'Little pop-eyes' was asleep and, oblivious of all moral values of work, he was snoring as loudly as any distinguished snoring mortal could. Kyanzo yanked the boy's head up and said, 'Don't sleep! Whoever became rich through sleep?'

I agreed with that. Nobody would, except in his dreams. Little Kyanzo woke up as he must have done on many occasions before, rubbed his eyes and squeaked that he was hungry.

'Hungry! You ate in the bus didn't you or are you worm-infested and you won't tell us?'

The little boy said nothing and, like his mother, stared at the fire as if some benevolent spirit would rise from it and feed them surreptitiously. Overhead the thunder rumbled, and the rain came down with renewed vigour. Soon the whole house was leaking, sending down dirty, brown drops upon our neat arrangement. Seeing this, Kyanzo began a tirade against the man who placed those things *there*, and the man who so poorly thatched the roof, and I believe that he would have gone on to blame the rain and the Beautiful Power behind the downpour, hadn't religion trained him to limit all his attacks to mankind in general but except himself. But while he railed, his wife and Hamad were busy moving the bed and all the household goods to the exact position they had been, before he gave the orders to change them. Upon seeing this the master said that that was the position in which they should have been kept in the first place and that he wondered at the idiot that had placed them in such vulnerable positions.

Since then I have seen people of various categories. But I vouch never to have seen a man so full of contradiction and blame compounded by acute shortage of memory as my host.

Just as we finished with the re-arrangement, the cock crowed. Hamad and I were to make bedding of sorts among the builders, and give room to the owners of the house. And as we left, the boy seemed wide awake still and was staring at the glowing embers. And the last thing I remembered about that night was seeing little Kyanzo with his eyes popping wide open as ever, repeatedly nodding at the fire, as if the latter compelled him to agree with something that was most detrimental to him.

I had not slept long before the birds began twittering and dawn broke. The others were still asleep when I went outside. A slight mist lay low over the hills, which seemed darker than usual and, except for the twittering of the birds and the perpetual roar of the river far below our house, the whole atmosphere was both quiet and unusually peaceful. I descended to the brook to wash my face. A surprise awaited me there. The small pool where I had bathed so often was no more. Instead, a huge projection of a horizontal rock lay across the widened stream; and, below it, a deep furrow cut its way vertically down to the main river far below. The muddy water cascaded over this projection and fell unimpeded at least seven metres to the next level of the stream below. Something that I couldn't define was changed. And in the roar of the falling waters, I derived some unease in my young heart. It was as if, like the pool, my heart itself had been emptied of its peace and quiet and was now being torn asunder. I washed my face in the muddy flowing water and went back to the house where my host-family lay.

The woman was there, standing beside the house and looking at the beautiful morning as if she could not see it; as if the whole sharply defined landscape was one mass—dark and indistinguishable. I bid her a good morning as cheerfully as I could and was highly disconcerted by her utter lack of concern. She did not return my greeting, but turning towards me, she fixed her eyes upon me—and stared at me as if I were a being newly arrived from outer space. They were vacant eyes—like a python's. Unnerved, I said 'Good morning.' And now a flicker of life passed across her face and she said, 'Yes, good morning,' in a far away, flat voice.

I was to get no breakfast for the master of the house was still asleep and something told me that from then henceforth, I shouldn't ask for food but should wait till it was quietly handed to me. So I tip-toed into the house, picked up my school bag and was soon on my way to school.

When I got to the river, I found that the makeshift, bridge had been swept away and that there was no trace of it ever having been there. Before me the river was one flowing mass of brown water. It was a fascinating sight and I found myself musing about the contradictions of nature: if I got into that river now, that would be the end of me. And yet in a few hours to come, an ant would cross along its sandy floor with impunity. Then my mind turned upon my hostess—and that blank face which had as little expression as the sheet of water before me. I realized for the first time that she did not yet have a name and her little dull-staring son had no name . . . Nameless people . . . As anonymous as this water.

Suddenly a hand was gently laid upon my shoulder and I turned. Hamad was there, smiling at me, his eyes seeming to read my thoughts and understand them.

'You left early today little teacher,' he said.

'Mm—Yes. I . . ., I wanted to see the river.'

'I know.'

A pause followed. We both contemplated the flowing river.

'What is her name?'

'Who?'

'She. At the house. Mr. Kyanzo's wife.'

Hamad was silent for a little while.

'Eileen,' he said.

'Eileen—what? I mean hasn't she got another name?'

'What other name?' asked Hamad, perplexed.

'I mean . . . my name is Joseph Kituku. What's her other name—the African one?'

'I don't know. All the time I've served them I've always known her as Eileen. Not that I have ever called her by it. Far from it. I'd be lost if I did.'

'How long have you been their servant?' I asked.

'Well . . . er . . . let me see . . . This is now the third year. I joined them when their son was two years old.'

'And where did you meet them? I mean, how did you meet them?'

'It's a long story and you mustn't be late for school . . . I'll tell you later maybe when you come back in the evening.'

'But I can't get to school anyway. Not across this river. So . . . '

'But I have to get back to work. I can't afford not to work.'

'Only the beginning then. And you can tell me the rest when I come back.'

And Hamad began:

'Before Mr. Kyanzo found me, I was a labourer at the farm of Bwana Mnazi Mkavu—yes—we all called him Bwana Mnazi Mkavu because he was very tall and straight, like the pole of a coconut tree. He was not a good man and flogged us workers as often as he pleased. People said he was a Boer, a settler from South Africa where the White settlers ate people . . . '

'Ate!' I asked, incredulous.

'Well, that's what the people said. But whether they ate people or not the fact remained that generally all the Boer settlers were more cruel than the other types. They seemed to enjoy seeing the blood of their servants flow and no one would rise up against them. Why?— I don't know. Once the D.O. of our area arrested one of them for nearly flogging a labourer to death and the D.O. never repeated that again—the next day he turned up all bruised and bloody to re-arrest the settler. And the settler came out with a shotgun and said any man who sympathised with a native ought to die. That's what happened in his homeland. So the D.O. backed down and left, threatening to bring justice upon the settler. Justice never came.'

Hamad reflected and continued. 'They were a cruel lot, those Boers—and were greatly feared. But in all our neighbourhood, no one was as feared as the man I served—this Bwana Mnazi Mkavu. He never saw you stand to stretch your back without coming down hard upon you with the whip. And many of us were sure to get whipped at least once a week.'

68

'You too?' I asked.

'Yes,' he replied calmly, 'me too. And like the others I put up with it. Had to keep my job. Then one day, a young girl came running into the farm, shouting in terror and waving her hands in the air. All of us labourers stopped working to look at her. And all this while, she was getting nearer towards us. Then the man next to me recognized her and, throwing down his hoe, ran to meet her crying, "Sister! Sister! what's the matter?" But before she reached us, Bwana Mnazi Mkavu intercepted her and struck her head with the butt of the rifle he had been hunting with. She fell down. But she didn't stay there. She tried to rise, and I saw the blood oozing from the nostrils. Mnazi Mkavu hit her again. And again. She tried to rise and crawl towards her brother with her hand outstretched, calling his name. Beside me, the brother stood, transfixed in fear. The girl crawled right up to his feet and clung to his knees, gasping, "Brother . . . Mother . . . Mother's dying . . . " And all this time, Mnazi Mkavu followed her, seeming to enjoy her pain, till she clung to her brother's knees. And then he hit her again and she fell. I jumped to her aid then, without knowing what I did. I picked her up and she lay, limp in my arms. Dead. And as her brother and I lay her body down, Mnazi Mkavu struck me with the butt of his rifle, drawing the blood from the back of my head. I lost all reasoning then and hit him. I put all my strength behind that blow and broke his jaw. And then I saw him lying there beside the girl and suddenly it occurred to me that there was not a single difference between them. Both of them had bodies made from the same earth. Both of them were capable of dying. Why then had he killed her when she tried to forestall her own mother's death? What made his life more precious, more superior to hers? Wasn't she also human? The fury with which I asked myself these questions blinded all my reasoning—and as Mnazi Mkavu regained consciousness, I could not bear to see him stir with life beside the innocent girl he had killed. And so I took his own gun and hit his head again and again, until I could no longer see the colour difference between the two heads—All I saw was the blood from the two human heads. And there was no difference . . . little teacher—there was no difference. The blood was RED in both of them.'

'You killed . . .!' I gasped '*You* a murderer?'

'Yes. I killed him,' he replied barely above a whisper.

Hamad was silent. And, like him the air was silent. Only the river murmured slightly—as its floods swept past us. Looking into the river, his face a set mask of conviction, he shook his fist at the river and, barely audibly talked to the waters, 'Go now and tell them I am here and I killed him and would do it again and again. He had no right—none whatever!'

He was silent again—and for a long time he gazed into the river as if he expected it to answer him. But the river flowed on, muddy and unheeding. At length he looked up and, looking at his face I noticed that there were tears there, large clear beads of tears chasing one after another down his cheeks and he, unaware of them, continued with his story:

'The girl lay there . . . dark and innocent as the earth on which she lay, and I stopped to pick her up. Her limp body was in my arms again and I turned to give it to her brother, but he had fled. Everyone had run away and I was left alone with the body in that endless farm. Then I saw a large cloud of dust

70

approaching and I knew that Mnazi Mkavu's son was coming for him, for the sun was high overhead. I placed the body of the dead girl over that of Mnazi Mkavu and ran.

'I ran the remainder of that day across the country in a northerly direction, avoiding the road and the railway. I even avoided the path lest they followed me and saw my footsteps.

'At night I camped high up in the branches of the tallest tree I could find. At dawn of the following day I came down from the tree and continued my journey northwards. I did not know where I was going and didn't care so long as I lengthened the distance between me and that farm. I hurried on until at about noon of that day, I came upon a large river and decided to sit upon its bank to rest. But it was not long before I heard, from a long way off, the barking of dogs which grew louder and louder and I knew I had been followed. I plunged into the river and let it carry me. For a long time I drifted along and meandered with the current across the plains. At one point I crossed the railway line where the river went under the bridge. Still I drifted, till I saw the road. I hid under the bridge and lay there for the night. No one had followed me for I neither heard any barking of dogs nor saw anybody. Except for the vehicles that roared past above me, the whole jungle lay silent. Then I had an idea: if I removed my shirt and let it drift downstream, perhaps my pursuers might pick it up and give me up for dead. It was that that saved me.

'Early the following morning, I resumed my northward trek, keeping to the bushes but close to the road. In the afternoon of that day I came upon a small market where I went to get some water. Here I learned that the news of the two deaths had spread, that the police had been placed on the alert, and that a search party had been sent to follow my trail. I was very hungry, but I dare not show it lest someone suspected me and began to ask questions. Just before I left, someone arrived in a lorry. And as his turnboys unloaded the vegetables, the driver strode over to where the market women were gathered and began to talk to them. He seemed to be a favourite of theirs for they laughed and joked with him. I was about to turn and leave the village when I heard one of the women ask whether there was any news of the murderer. The man said that it was over.

"Over?" I asked.

"Yes."

'Apparently the search-party had not given up, but knowing that I could not have crossed that flooded river, they must have deduced that I had to look for the bridge. So they followed me downstream where they saw my shirt dangling from a tree branch over a waterfall. Then they took the shirt and argued that I must be dead for no one would outlive the series of falls below that branch.

'The man ended his story by saying that he would give anything to have me as his friend, that the settler deserved such treatment as I had given him and that he himself would have done no less. He highly commended my action and said that such men as my former master should be exterminated for robbing our people of the land which had belonged to them for generations untold. In short, he praised my action to such an extent that by the time he left, I felt I was a hero. Any fear that I had felt was completely gone. And from that moment, I was determined to seek that man out, for I felt that my hope of a new life lay with him. From this conversation, I gathered that he was going up north to the town of Ngotheni, where he had a shop. When he had left, I asked one of the women who the man was. She seemed surprised that I didn't know Kyanzo, that I must be a stranger if I didn't, for Kyanzo was the sole supplier of all the vegetables from the coast up north to the end of the road; Kyanzo was the richest known African in those areas. His riches were surpassed by neither chief nor headman but only by the white men. Even some white men respected him as some other women commented. I asked where his home was, and I was told that he mostly lived at Ngotheni but that he had a home somewhere in the country but they didn't know where. When I left the women I enquired after Ngotheni and the man I asked said that it was a whole half-day's journey by rail. That decided it. I was determined to catch the train at the next station that same evening. I took to the bush again and walked for some distance. Then I came upon a homestead, near which some lambs played. I crept nearer, grabbed one of these and ran into the bush.'

'You stole!' I exclaimed.

'Do you think I wanted to?' he asked in fury. 'I had to live, little teacher. I had to live! And that was the only way.

'I dared not make a fire. So I ate the meat raw. I continued my journey and arrived at the station late in the afternoon. And for the rest of that day, I lay low until the train arrived.

'It came just after sunset. At first the engine thundered by; then came the long clean well-polished first class compartments which, I knew, were always reserved for the white people. I saw their faces flash by and never once did I see more than two faces looking out of the same window. And I still remember them: calm and contented faces, looking out with interest and happiness into the darkening land. Then the second class compartments rattled by, and through the windows I saw the faces of Asians mostly—talking to their fellows on the seats opposite. And then followed a long processsion of dark long compartments, served with innumerable windows. And out of each window a swarm of black heads fought for space to catch the view of their own land—a swarm of bees doomed to move out in search of new flowers, without a place to rest and call home—for there was nowhere in all this land they could call home. Everything belongs to foreign crowns abroad as you very well know, little teacher. A man builds a house on a piece of land. A foreign boy of twenty admires it, and his 'Mother-crown' back home ratifies his claim of ownership. The boy decides that he'll turn this home into a holiday resort, locks it up and goes back to mother-crown and boasts about his development projects out there in his new country. And now the original owner passes by, fighting for space enough to catch a glimpse of the place where his home used to be.

'I fought the crowds that waited upon the pavement and . . . well . . . I *am* strong you know, so I got first position up the stairs and into the crowded compartment. It was full! And I wondered how so small a place could hold so many people, let alone the piles of luggage that blocked the gangway. So I stood near the door, risking being thrown out when the train jolted and clanged out of the station. From what a fellow-passenger told me, we would reach Ngotheni at cock-crow, and that there were many stations between this and my final destination. But I did not

74

accept his advice that I should sleep, because I didn't have any money for my fare and had to be on the look-out for the ticket-examiner. We passed two stations before anything happened. Then there were loud and hoarse whispers that the ticket examiner was coming. I saw him, cursing and battling with the piles of luggage in the gang-way as he slowly made his way towards me, examining tickets. When he reached the centre of the compartment, I dived into the lavatory and stayed there for a long time. Someone banged the door and told me to open and upon her receiving no answer, either in word or deed, she asked what I was doing in there. Then I quickly opened the door and apologised for my severe diarrhoea. The woman told me that the shakings and rattlings of *this* end of the train was enough to give anyone diarrhoea, be he our big bellied Governor of Her Majesty's Colony—or any hungry beggar within it. She further advised me to keep very near the door, for if one had diarrhoea, it was not safe to be far from the lavatory. After this we parted as amiably as would any two travellers who had very little to part with, either in this train or whither we were bound.

'The ticket examiner had passed, and I sighed with relief. But, before long, a train guard appeared, also re-examining tickets and, because the woman was still in the lavatory, I opened the door and crouched on the steps outside. The train was flying at great speed then and, as we rounded a bend so that I could clearly see the mighty arms of the engine as they propelled the wheels, I was badly jolted and would have fallen, had I not found a metal projection of the door-hinges and clung to it, till my fingernails were nearly ripped off. Someone coughed in the compartment further ahead, and the whole, dark, dense, stinking sputum landed *whack* upon my face, right here between my eyes and I was in great agony holding on to the hinges with five fingernails and scooping that mess off my face with the other hand. Nor was this all. We had not gone far before some stinking dishwater came, flying the whole length of the train, drenching me soundly. A mother up-ahead decided that her young child needed an urgent piss, and she simply stood that child at the open window, let it piss into the air, oblivious that I would be drenched with it further down the line. And by the time I decided that the guard had passed and I should go back inside, my body had been battered and soaked by an innumerable assort-ment of solids and liquids: from Indian curry-meat-balls to piss and white man's liquor so that I was obliged to remain in the lavatory perpetually, for my body and clothing stank heavily. Thus we travelled on, northwards, towards Ngotheni.

'The old man had been right. Just as the cock crowed from somewhere in the darkness, the train clanked into Ngotheni station. And what a station! There were rows of bright lights that stretched on and on so that I thought a section of the clear sky had fallen. At last the train stopped and, as you can ima-gine, I was the first to step on to the pavement. I dashed into the shadows and waited until the train had pulled out of the station. I remember looking at the red-lights of the guardian as they receded into the distance as if they were wishing me good luck.

'Very soon, the station was deserted and I was left standing in the shadows all by myself. My attention was attracted by a huge rubber tap looming over the rails directly before me. A sizable jet of clean water was flowing from it. Someone had forgotten to shut the tap tight after filling the last train. I decided to

76

have a shower. I couldn't appear before the man who admired me in this sorry state. So I marched over to the tap and stood under it, with all my clothes on, that we might both be washed clean. That water was cold! But I persevered. I *must* be clean! I let it drench me and I rubbed myself as best as I could.

'It was not long before one of the station guards noticed me and ran towards me.

' "Get away from this water, man! Are you crazy?" he asked me in Swahili. I replied that I was only having a shower and I would get away as soon as I had finished. The man took this as an affront to his intelligence and, coming near, he said, "I *know*! But this water was not meant for any stray vagabond or lost mongrel at Ngotheni station. It was meant for *trains* to drink! Now you haven't become a train by any chance have you?"

'I replied that it wasn't very likely.

' "Then scram! In the first place you are standing where the train should stand. The next one is due in three minutes. Now get moving!"

'But while he had been barking at me, I was busy scrubbing my clothes so that when I obeyed his orders, both my body and clothes were tolerably clean. I went back to my corner. But the guard would not entertain that. He probably thought I'd wage a battle with the next train for the use of the tap! So he chased me out of the station yard, out of the railway residential area, and into the bright streets beyond. Here I loitered to keep warm and help the water drip faster out of my clothes. I met quite a few beggars, some of whom laughed at my ridiculous clothing. But others were kinder and invited me to warm myself by their fire. To these people, I related my misfortune. And when I came to that of the things thrown at me on the train's steps, one among them observed that my plight that night paralleled their experience almost every night. For many were the nights when dishwater had been emptied on to their heads from many a rich kitchen far above them. But the fire and the conversation of these beggars did much to remove the numbness in my spirits so that I looked forward with hope to the breaking dawn.

'When it dawned, the day promised to be bright. I asked my friend whether they knew of a shopkeeper by the name of Kyanzo. They started in unison. Kyanzo—a shopkeeper! He was a lord if anything! He was the only black man that could dine with the white people—and that was a great achievement! He had a business; controlled all fruit and vegetable trade in Ngotheni. Why the Governor himself often bought fruit from Kyanzo's main shop. They wanted to know if I was a relation of his, and when I told them that I was merely an acquaintance, almost to a man, they told me it were better if he didn't know me—for *they* knew! But they would not say what they knew or why he shouldn't know me. I have been his servant for three years now and haven't found much to complain about except that he's too stern towards his wife and son.

'One of my new friends took me directly to Kyanzo's store, perhaps in the hope that I might remember him when I might see better days. It was a large building before which a number of cars were parked and out of which dogs and white and brown women came forth. I was rather worried that one of these women would recognize me and I waited until there was no customer before I dashed across the street and into his store.

'He was alone, or I thought he was alone because his wife, who sat obediently at the corner, did not stir when I came in. Kyanzo smiled broadly when he saw me and said that he was sure he had seen me before. I replied that he had—and the day was the one before.

' "Pardon me . . . I have such a bad memory for names but your name you said was Mr . . . er . . .?" said Kyanzo.

' "Muhamad."

' "Of course! Of course!—Muhammad! Must be a Moslem then?"

'I said I didn't have any religion particularly.

' "And you are boy to Mr . . . er . . . "

'I looked around before I answered and, except for his wife, who didn't seem interested in our conversation, there was no one in that store except Mr. Kyanzo and me.

' "Van—Den—Newt!"

' "Van—Den—Newt! The Boer settler? The one they called Mnazi Mkavu? The one who was murdered?"

' "The same."

' "And you are looking for a job now that your former master is dead? You did well. There's nothing better than a job. Keeps a man alive and full of purpose and drive . . . Do you, by any chance know exactly what happened to him?"

'I asked him to take me to somewhere quiet so that I might tell him. We went into an inner room. And there I told him everything: of Mkavu's cruelty, of the weeping young girl whom he had killed, of my killing him, and of my trek up country—and ended with the hope that he would help me as he had implied in front of the women the day before.

'Kyanzo was quiet for a long time. And when he spoke, I felt that he had lost a little of his charm. He told me that he would take me to a place where I would be well hidden, a place that was far from the settlers and the police. And in return for his protection I would work for him.'

'Without pay?' I asked.

'Without pay. But what is pay against one's life?' said Hamad. 'I have been here for three years now and I don't have much to complain about. You see—little teacher—I have no one left. All I had, my parents and my sister, are gone. My life means nothing to anyone except myself and when I follow them, I will have left nothing to anyone. And so I work and work for another day to buy my life.'

I felt a pang of sadness rip through me, for I loved him as my elder brother. And, for lack of better words with which to express myself, I cried indignantly, 'That's not true! That's not true! If you left me you'll have left . . . you'll have left . . .' But I couldn't quite define what he would have left.

'There you are . . . little teacher . . . Even you, who have taught me, will have lost nothing,' he said, and I did not dissuade him from that point, for he seemed stuck fast in his grief. I thought his voice was breaking and looked up at his face. I see that face before me now after these many years. It rises before me like the rock on which his foot rests—his eyes have a far-away look as if he sees right through the hills and out into space. Slowly the eyes moisten and he comes back to earth; the face softens; he wipes his eyes once and says, 'Anyway, that's how I first met Kyanzo and came into his employment.'

While he was telling his story, the river had been falling. Now large boulders began to show and the water cascaded over them down into a wide expanse of calm surface below. And as the waters subsided, the roar of the river increased—so that I barely heard the tolling of the bell from the Mission School. The mist had risen, sending thin strands of cloud wafting across the sky. The sun now peeped briefly through them and I was astonished at how late it was. Still the waters raged and I dared not cross. Then Hamad had an idea. Further upstream, there was a point where the river narrowed. This place was overlaid with large creepers and climbing plants. We would use them to cross the river.

We went upstream and presently came upon the spot. The creepers and climbers were there all right but did not overlie the river. Instead, they grew up the thick trees on each side of the river bank. Hamad swung into action. Climbing up the trees, he unfurled two of the long thick tendons of the creepers and began to twine them as we did ropes back at home. I looked on, amazed at the speed with which he worked, and marvelled at the strength of his hands as the twine of climbers furled and unfurled at the sharp, sudden twists of his muscles. Soon he made a 'rope', long enough to cross the whole width of the river. Then he climbed up the tree, and high up the branches, he fastened it.

He came down the vine, hand over hand and tugging it to test and strengthen its hold on the branch. Soon he was on the ground, satisfied with his work. And, with me holding him tight around the middle we swung clean across the roaring waters and landed clear on to the opposite bank.

'There you are, little teacher.'

Then he gave me the only fifty cents I knew he possessed and told me to use that instead of the breakfast I had missed. Then swinging himself across the river like a friendly gorilla, he landed safely on the other side. I watched him pick his way among the trees back to the home where Kyanzo dictated his life. Then I left that spot and walked down the river bank. The little sweet potato gardens that had safely lain beside the river, had been swept clean away. And as I walked down the bank, I picked some of the stray potatoes abandoned among the debris. These I ate as I picked my way to school.

I found that I was very late. As I entered our class-room, the headmaster appeared around the corner, ready to give us another dose of his Rural Science. And as I dodged along the rows of desks (most of which were empty) I wondered what Rural Science would say to *this* storm. I was apprehensive that the first thing he would do would be to call me out in front and cane me. But he did no such thing. Instead, he bolted into the room—smiling! And the first thing he said after beaming 'Good morning class' was to ejaculate:

'Ah, What rain! What rain!' Upon which he set down his books, clapped his two soft hands, rubbed them together and observed that 'not all my children are here!' To which the class monitor (the little rogue who had told me I was not clever at everything) said, 'They did not come to school—sir, because of the rain, sir—They would not come until the afternoon—sir!' All of this the headmaster seemed to take with the air of the benign parent of yesterday who would not cane his son, and he said that they would come when the Lord chose to reduce the waters. After this we embarked upon Rural Science, and for the first time since he undertook to instruct us in this subject, I enjoyed it immensely. No longer the study of granites underlying all those hills to the west of the school; no more the dry recitations of the parts of the tree, the life history of the praying mantis (whose attitude we had thoroughly copied), no more the headmaster standing still and stiff and, like a bad oracle, spewing out monotonous and sonorous speeches about the horrors of the locust, the house-fly, the ichneumuon fly (I liked *that* name!). No. This day we talked about the Rain! and the effect of Rain on all things. And before my very eyes, the little headmaster came down the whole ladder of Authority, threw away the ladder, steel rungs and all, and, on that floor, became one of us. For the rest of that class, we were treated to all the delicacies available in any kind of Rural Science one cared to mention.

The lesson was upon the subject of the germination of seeds; and he taught it in the form of a story. Long ago there was a seed drying in the parched soil. Here he made two pupils come out to the front and he told them that they were suffering and drying up in the soil. Hesitantly, the two little boys stood in front of us, squatted facing one another and as they began to live up to the story, they became those 'dicotyledons' and I never saw any two creatures suffer as did those dicotyledons, as they waited for the rain. As I watched I thought I saw them evade both fire and the cane.

The teacher was speaking.

'Then God decided to send heavy rain upon it and the seed swelled out with pleasure . . .'

He had the class prefect come out to administer this divine blessing. And to this day I still remember this devil of a bad-tempered bully, having to change and be kind enough to bring us rain. But rain he did bring to the seed and what with the class clapping and encouraging him, he did such a fine job of it that by the time he had finished with his mission of mercy, I am sure that the Benevolent One above us was all smiles that any mortal could thus duplicate and acknowledge His Goodness. The seed began to swell and the cotyledons swelled to such a degree that I thought nothing matched this fullness save advanced pregnancy. Then they decided to 'grow' and bring forth a tiny little leaf (which they did with the aid of their hands); with their legs the primary root was shot down into the soil and I thought that soil was very wet for the root had a very easy time of it as he shot into the ground.

Thus Rural Science that day. It was so vivid and so enjoyable that when exams came and we were asked to write the whole story of the germination of seeds, God came into the Science and became the prime mover of the whole process, and only the propriety of modern learning forbade my drawing that Glad Old Man of the sky with his hands spread over all the earth—where the dry and miserable seeds of all that had life lay dying. His hands spread over all life— sending endless gentle rain upon us all.

I was in great amazement as to the cause of this miraculous transformation of our headmaster until the class monitor, (who always brought to us all the latest gossip as any mongrel did fleas) said to me in the manner of one who knew I was one rung below him, for I *didn't* know everything.

'Don't you know? His wife had a baby boy last night and his three acre garden wasn't washed away by the rain as happened to all the surrounding gardens!' I was opening my mouth and continuing to say that he was a very blessed man when this little brat of cold waters dampened my vision and said, 'Nonsense! Everyone knows that his wife went to a white man's hospital, and his garden is all terraced by twenty servants.'

Still I felt that it was a strange coincidence that the rain should have touched down first upon this school, that the headmaster was visited on this night with twin blessings, that he should be changed enough to forgive late-comers, and that he should conduct the most interesting lesson I had ever had from him. In my simple child's mind, and out of my strict religious upbringing in which hope always featured prominently, I concluded that the heart of this man was greatly changed and that the boys of Kyambe School were sure to see better days. But I was sadly disabused when a week later, we reverted to the old Rural Science. Now we were forced to draw the human skeleton and recite all its parts. And in the drought of this lesson, my mind wandered into all sorts of speculations; what would happen if those glaring skeleton teeth began to talk to one another, whether the digits of hands and feet were secure enough and wouldn't crack and pop off the paper as did our dry castor oil seeds, and fly into the headmaster's face with a vengeance. I even entertained hopes of seeing the whole skeleton come dancing to school and wondered what punishment our headmaster would mete out—whether he would command the skeleton to go back to the graveyard, dig up its mother and appear before the judgement of us all; and whether or not the offspring skeleton would be punished with a wooden cane. In the absurdity of this skeletal image being whipped and yelping and prancing about in pain, I found so much to laugh at, that I could no longer contain it and I burst out laughing, to the utter amazement of the whole class—a thing which earned me twelve strokes of the cane after school, and in the house of Correction.

But, save for this interesting lesson on germination, the day was dull, both in the following classes and out in the very air we breathed. Overhead, the sky was dull and overcast and no wind blew. As I went home that evening, it was still dull, humid, and uncomfortable. When the Rural Science class was over, my mind reverted to Hamad and I tried, without success to be reconciled to the idea that this man, out of whom goodness bubbled like the clear waters of the spring, had *murdered a man*. This contradiction occupied my mind as I walked home, hungry, under that silent and dull sky. I now came upon the river at the point where the bridge used to be. The boulders had all been fully uncovered and only a small stream of water branched out between them. But, far below the boulders, the torrent of the storm had dug out a wide plunge-pool that ate deep into the river banks so that the foliage of the trees hovered above it like the fingers of so many angry ghosts. A strange fear gripped me. It was all so ghostly silent except for the rippling water that trickled into the wide plunge-pool, murmuring incessantly as if it was trying to tell a story it had told so many times before but hadn't yet mastered it enough to say where the story came from. I hastened across the boulders—on towards home.

There was no one about when I arrived. The door was locked and, save for a large green fly that buzzed around me as if it had become the guard of this house and was come to ask what my business was upon those premises, nothing else moved. It was silent, more silent than the pool. I trudged up to the main house but this too was deathly quiet. I called out the name of the head-builder but only the echo came back to me, from all sides of the house. Then it was silent again; heavily silent. A slight breeze passed by and somewhere up above, a loose iron sheet rattled dully and then it was silent again. Weird cracking sounds emanated from all over the roof, punctuating the silence like perplexed ghosts. I grew uneasy and walked out of the house and down to the much simpler one. I was so hungry and dejected that I didn't feel any urge to go looking for my hosts. So I just sat on a small embankment beside the house, and waited.

Five

How long I sat there I do not remember. All I recollect is that I dozed intermittently and that, when I decided to stand up and stretch my legs, the sun had set over everything except the highest hill-tops. Looking at the sky, large brown shafts of sunlight seemed to grow from over our hill and explode into nothingness in the sky above me.

Then I saw them. They were coming up the hill from the direction of the garden, all silent. With a large new hoe flung over his shoulder, Hamad was in front. His head was bent down upon the path he had trodden so many times before. He, too, was silent. Behind him, Eileen whose other name had been forbidden her, trudged on and she was as silent as she had been that morning. The load of firewood strapped upon her back seemed to add weight to the silence. The little boy lagged two terraces behind. On his back was strapped a basket which swayed to and fro and with which movement the boy complied, so that he zigzagged up the path and knocked his feet and stumbled against the irregular mounds of debris that the storm had created. At one time he stood still and surveyed the country around him as if he expected some benevolent spirit to come from the sky and help him. Then he interlocked both hands upon his head and burst into tears.

When he heard the cry, Hamad turned, and laying down his hoe, he strode down to the boy and with one hand he took the load off his back. At this, the boy's shrill wails died down to a whimper and then stopped altogether. Eileen walked on, and to this day, I am convinced that she did not hear the cry of her son. The son now walked close behind Hamad as if the latter was guardian against a terrible beast close behind him. When they reached the spot where Hamad had left his hoe, Hamad bent down to pick it up. And as he lifted it, the boy stretched out his hand. Hamad gave it to him and I thought that even though he did not smile, the boy carried that hoe with great pleasure. When he reached me, he struck it upon the ground with as much force as he was master of, as if he would bury once and for all the terrible beast that had lurked at his heels. I did not see Kyanzo and I scanned the darkening landscape for signs of him so that I might prepare myself against his hardness. But I did not see him. And for the time being, I was free and greatly relieved.

That evening, when Eileen busied herself by the fire as she prepared our supper, Hamad and I occupied ourselves with books. I was teaching Hamad the art of simple addition in arithmetic and I thought I would never have a worse pupil. He had this bad habit of adding by counting, which made me fly into fits of unreasoning rage. I would tell him that one plus one equals two, and write it down for him. Then he would write it down for himself but not before he had lifted his left forefinger, then his right, brought them together and then murmured, 'one, two,' before he wrote the answer. Gradually he lost most of the urge to add by counting like a little child, and began to add automatically on paper. All went very well until we got to adding five and seven. By the unconscious addition formula that I had implanted within him, he got the answer right and he wrote down twelve. Then he inclined his head and looked askance at that number and I thought it had greatly offended him, so I asked, 'Well . . . What is it?'

'It's not right!' he said.

'Of course it's right,' I said confidently and then by way of encouragement, 'You are doing very well indeed, progressing very fast.' But Hamad continued to be quizzical about it all.

'No! The whole idea is stupid!' he said suddenly.

'What *are* you talking about? Five plus seven equals twelve. And *you* have got it right—down *here*! What are you complaining about?' I retorted, thinking that like his master's wife and son, something had gone wrong.

'I *know* that five and seven make twelve. But then what do they define? They are just numbers. They mean nothing!'

The man is raving mad, I thought.

'I mean if you say one hoe and another one hoe make two hoes, that's more correct . . . a little more meaningful.'

'Oh, I see! Call it what you like. Five men and seven men . . . Anything!' I said.

Hamad was silent for a while, in which time he managed to chew all the rubber at the other end of his pencil.

'That is still not right. It is not true!'

'Well . . . Why not?' I screeched angrily.

'It still does not define anything! Surely one hoe plus another hoe doesn't make *two* hoes. A hoe might be big or small. Now a big hoe plus a small hoe doesn't add up to two hoes. If they do, you are assuming that we are just adding the *idea* of hoes and not *real* hoes, hoes I can touch and feel; hoes I can dig with. And if you are just dealing with the idea of hoes and totally neglect *their use*, what use is your arithmetic? Don't you see?' he said appealingly. But I couldn't see the logic behind such confusion—and I said so.

Hamad went on.

'Why, it's so simple! If you told me to go to the shop and buy you two hoes, surely you wouldn't just end there. The message would be incomplete. Why? Because you have failed to tell me what type of hoes; how big, how long, how thick the handles. And why do you have to tell me all this? Because I will be looking for a particular hoe which I will use for a particular function. A hoe I'd use to dig soft ground would not be the same hoe as I would use to dig a stony area. It must be an *individual* hoe that you'll ask me to buy, else you'd be very irresponsible; if you asked me to bring *any* two hoes without giving me strict definitions about them, I might bring you the strangest combination you ever did see—and I am sure you'd not be pleased. You see?'

I hotly replied that such intricacies couldn't get into arithmetic, else we'd all end up in a mess. Imagine what would happen if I had to define every one of four million articles and every one of three

become a mass, and have let people rule us as a mass just because we are grown up, beats all my senses.'

I said nothing, for I didn't quite follow what he had been saying, or what black men, mass, Jones, Jennifer, Mwanamama and all the rest of them, had to do with either me or arithmetic. So I just nodded to hide the fact that I had long become muddled, and to act as an understanding teacher, else I would soon lose a pupil. For one of the most valuable lessons I had learned up the academic tree was that, a teacher must always be wiser than his pupil. But Hamad still had a complaint and he went on.

'Not long ago just before you were born, there was a very big war. I learned that a man called Hitler decided that other men did not have a right to live in peace and in their own land. So he just marched upon them and harassed them out of their lands, and many, out of their lives. Why? Because he looked over all earth and didn't see anyone there. He just saw a *mass* of bodies. And since you can't make any sense out of a mass of bodies, he couldn't either. (Well—he was human like you and me). So he just went there and mauled them just as a plough mauls a piece of earth— because it's just an anonymous mass of clay. If that man saw individuals there, the chances are that he would see himself as an individual and realize he could not and should not maul them off the earth. Men like that, see too late that there *were* individuals after all and they learn only by pain, as did that dict- ator in the big war. And they are no better than the beasts of the field. For only animals learn through pain. No knowledge is worth anything if it was forced and pained into you. And it all begins because every- thing, including people, is just an idea—like your arithmetic. And you resort to making ideas of things that are simple and easy to see because you can't really see them. And you can't see them because you can't face them. If you look at a hoe, *that* hoe, then another hoe would not be the same. What happened at that farm happened because Mnazi Mkavu—an individual, could not see any one of us, we were all an amorphous mass of easily dispensable black people. So I won't sit here and learn something that will lead me into lies—because I'm not a liar, and a liar is the stupidest thing I know.'

Thus he ended. Thus ended Hamad and arithmetic. I did not understand it or his hatred of what he called 'an idea'. And I must say that up till now, I have not been able to follow his argument. He suggested that I should give him another lesson on how to read and write, and despite my fear that he would tear my lesson apart, I began to instruct him and he delved in it with his eyes, mind and soul.

All this time Eileen was cooking and at the time when Hamad's explanation was getting too complicated for me to understand, I cast covert glances at my hostess. There she sat, still in the same position, stirring the pot with exactly the same circular movements and at exactly the same speed, and I thought she was utterly unaware of this world. But she *was* aware. When Hamad got angry, burst out, and raised his voice above normal, I thought I saw her shoulders bunch up, the wooden spoon remain tense in her hands for brief moments and her whole body stiffen. Otherwise she remained gloomy and cooked the food mechanically. And I wondered what kind of dish she would offer us in the end.

And all this while young Kyanzo's eyes popped at the fire. Sometimes, especially when Hamad was working at his writing, I saw him fix those blank eyes upon the exercise book, as if the spell he seemed to be under, had something to do with that book. Presently Hamad looked up from his writing and, catching young Kyanzo in the act of staring, said, 'Come, come, come and read with me, eh!'

The boy rose up mechanically and, with his left fore-finger shyly in his mouth, making an opening through which saliva drooled on to his shirt, he stood by Hamad's knee. Both seemed unaware of the saliva that now drooled on to the knee. The boy stood there, hesitantly until Hamad slapped his knee and motioned him to sit there. The boy dropped, but, halfway down, he seemed to get the idea that the knee was either dangerous or too sacred to be his seat and he straightened up with an alacrity I had not yet seen him show. Hamad pulled him on to his knee, where the boy now sat and, together, they read (or Hamad read to the boy, until the boy, now more confident, removed that finger from his mouth and with it, helped Hamad trace the sentences along the pages of the exercise book.

It was such a harmonious sight to see that I rose, in order to see those forefingers, the one large, dark and stubby, the other thin, anaemic-brown and long, going left to right and back again to left and then to right, like two bulls of different generations ploughing rather stony land. Along each sentence, Hamad would pronounce the last word loudly and in a high exclamatory tone of finality, as if he had not been sure of seeing the end of the line and by good luck he had unexpectedly stumbled upon it. At first, the boy kept him company with his forefinger. But as Hamad's reading and exclamations became more familiar and the boy more confident, he began to imitate the rhythm. And for the rest of that evening

I sat and watched and listened to them. At the end of each sentence, their voices would rise, that of the boy coming half a beat before, and ending half a beat after Hamad's. They read on to the end of the page and turned over a new leaf. Feeling that he was really winning this game, the boy grew so confident and so jubilant that he chuckled at the end of each line and Hamad said, 'We'll make you the best scholar in this country yet!' to which the boy nodded vigorously, and smiling, said, 'Yes'—though I guessed it was not the idea of the highest scholarship in our country that appealed to him as much as that a grown-up was there, having a game with him, letting him win as many times as he pleased, gaining confidence in a new sense of belonging.

I was so absorbed in what the scholars did that I forgot all about Eileen. When I looked in her direction again, I almost gasped. The pot was now off the fire and she was sitting still, looking at the three of us like one spellbound. What I remember most about her as I travel back to that night is her eyes. And I still see them, not dull, dead and lifeless now, but alive, as live as the embers that glowed below her. Once, when I tended goats in our pastures I had concentrated so heavily on a grass basket I was making that I forgot all about the goats until, jumping out of the world of making, to that of my irresponsibility to the herd, I suddenly looked up—right into the dark eyes of a gigantic leopard, eyeing me with curiosity. I did not start outwardly then, but the shock I felt was so gripping that it coursed down every nerve in my body and left me as one transfixed or frozen. It was this kind of shock my body registered when I suddenly found this woman's eyes upon us. At about the same time as I did, Hamad and young Kyanzo looked up

96

too. Then she looked down into the fire, and I thought I saw a smile flicker across her small mouth, though of that, I am not sure.

She dished out the food and I began to change my mind about this woman. The meal was delicious and each of us three scholars finished his share. For my part I finished and licked my plate. Then I gave it to Eileen for more. For reply, she ran the wooden spoon around the insides of the pot, making very strange noises in there as if she called the pot to witness that she was telling the truth, that the pot was empty and there was no more! She seemed to think this method of communication an ingenious and highly original device of hers and she smiled with satisfaction. Hamad laughed outright at this and little Kyanzo followed and laughed so shrilly I thought a happy weaver bird had come among us, and this was so tickling and pleasant to hear that both Eileen and I burst out laughing. All of us were laughing, and I could barely catch Hamad's words that came through the laughter.

'Greedy! Gree . . . he-he-iddy ha-ha-ha-Te-hehe-cher!' Over, near the fireplace, Eileen's mouth was open, displaying white, even teeth; her eyes were shut tight and turned up to heaven. Beads of tears rolled down her cheeks and on to her chest and her whole body was stiff and shaking with the paroxysm of laughter that rippled with it. The fire too, seemed to catch the disease and join in the fun for suddenly it glowed, setting alight the embers that had been smoking. I felt a cold wisp of wind sear across the back of my neck. Simultaneously Eileen's eyes opened and I saw her stiffen and sit mute, like a cornered sheep before a devouring leopard. The laughter died as suddenly as it had begun and I turned. The door stood wide open and, standing before it, with his black crumpled hat still upon his head, was Kyanzo. I looked up at his face once and didn't dare to look upon it again. Even as I write, I still see his large eyes, glowing like balls of fire as he surveys the four of us like the very personification of the last judgement.

'Well . . . Go on! Laugh! Why do you stop?' No one answered him. No one laughed. Silence.

'Eileen, what was it all about?'

'Well' . . . stammered Eileen, but could not finish. I decided to speak.

'It was I.'

'What about you?' Kyanzo snapped.

'Well . . . I wanted some more food and there wasn't any more. So we laughed.'

'Is that enough reason to bellow out loud, eh? Eileen? Is that how I taught *you* to be head of this home while I'm away? Eh? I turn my back for two minutes and what do I find? The head of *my* home laughing and joking with servants and children! Is that how you will behave when I have gone back to Ngotheni? Tell me *is* that how?' he roared, striding across to her.

'Is that how you will care for *my* property eh? *Is that how*?' he screeched, orchestrating each of the last three syllables with a slap across her face, sending her face in the opposite direction with each slap. Eileen now cried and fresh tears of pain now gathered upon her eyelashes, which dropped with her bent head. And I watched them gather over her lower eyelids and drop; one drop after another, down on to the ashes.

'Is that how I taught you to be an intelligent mother to *this* child, letting him *laugh* with his superiors which *you* know is bad manners?'

'N. . . no,' Eileen stammered feebly. And if any intelligent being walked into this house then, heard this weak voice and saw the weakling that made it, he would have disproved that answer outright. But Kyanzo seemed to be satisfied with this answer and directed his barbs at me.

'And *you*! Why were you transferred to Kyambe School?'

'To study.'

'And what have you been doing?' he asked. And I thought his words would coil around my neck and stifle me to death—so cold they were, like the cold glitter of a python's coil.

'We had been studying and . . .'

'We?'

'Yes. Hamad sometimes . . .' I began.

'Hamad! Study? What *are* you talking about?'

'Well . . . I teach him to read and . . .'

'Teach? Since when did *you* become a teacher? And who gave *you* authority to teach him?'

Hamad sat silently through all this—he who was so strong and could easily break every bone of this lanky tyrant sat, silent, withdrawn into himself and staring at the floor.

'Nobody allowed me,' I said.

'And when do you find time to teach him?'

'In the evenings, after supper.'

'Don't you have enough school work to do?'

'I have.'

'Did you have any today?'

'Yes.'

'Have you done it?'

'No.'

'When were you going to do it?'

I kept silent. It was best.

'And how much does Hamad pay you?'

'Nothing.'

'Nothing? Don't lie to me. Hamad can lie and I wouldn't mind. He has no obligation not to. But you, Kituku, are a Christian, you come of a fine Christian home. Your father is one of the most honest straight-forward men I know. So don't *lie* to me. How much does he pay you?' Again the cold python wound its coils around me—and I was suffocating and freezing.

'Nothing!'

'Kituku, nobody ever does something for nothing. A man could accept something for doing nothing. Many beggars do. But nobody does something for no-thing. So don't lie to me. How much does he pay you? Or what does he pay you? . . .'

I didn't say anything. I could say nothing. I was lost in the contradiction between Hamad being a willling beggar and my having to get my pound of flesh like the man of Venice we had been told about in school . . . 'Perhaps an escort to the local dances? I hear you all go to dances at night,' continued Kyanzo. 'Or perhaps some lessons at guitar playing, so that you can become guitarist for the local dances? Don't deny it! The builders told me. Eh—is that it?'

I feebly agreed that sometimes Hamad taught me how to play the guitar.

'So that's it!' Pause. Then, 'Kituku go out and get me a good stick.'

I obeyed and returned with an eucalyptus stick.

'Stand there!' He ordered me. I obeyed, quaking before the deadly look in his eyes.

'Kituku, when your father asked me to give you shelter, he told me to treat you as his friend's son and as I would treat that son of mine there. Before your own eyes he gave me leave to punish you when occasion required it and I *am* going to cane you. Not because I hate you. No, on the contrary, I love you as my own son. But I hate the evil that is slowly creeping into you. And I will not stand by and see my friend's son, whom I love, go to ruin. Come here!'

I came nearer, quaking.

'I am going to chastise the evil of lies. You have told me lies tonight. And I am going to chastise the evil of joining wicked people to do wicked things and not doing your school work—which is why you were accepted under my roof.'

And he caned me! My God, he caned me! He caned me until the stick broke into smithereens and he ordered another one and yet another. I cried. I cried until I lost my voice; until I was bleeding from the face, hands, buttocks, legs and all over. When no voice came out, I still heard the voice of the others as they too cried with me. And as the maniac released me and I tottered to the floor, (he had a grip like an iron vice), I heard their wails. Of those wails, one rose higher than all the rest. And the agonized voice of that small boy has outlived all these years in which other men and women have cried in my presence. And to this day, as when I slid to the floor, I still see him, weak as he is and standing no higher than his father's thigh, fighting his father's legs with all the strength he can command—fighting a power that does not even feel the blow, so insignificant is it.

Hamad was looking down at me. Then I saw him turn towards Kyanzo. But I couldn't see him clearly. He seemed to expand and contract, like a man's reflection in the water and as I lost consciousness, I heard Kyanzo speak, like a loud trumpet far far above, 'Hamad! Don't you dare! Never dare to raise your hand against me nor ever think of it.'

And then I felt myself floating upon an endless mass of gentle water which bobbed me gently up and down, up and down, up and down to the tune of, 'think of it, think of it-it-it-it.'

When I regained consciousness, I was lying in Hamad's arms, facing the clear sky. Hamad was asking, 'Why' and then again, 'Why.' And the quarter moon that hung over the hill like a question mark, seemed to swim up and down as I viewed it through my tears, echoing Hamad and sending out the question 'Why' across the clear starry sky and beyond, across the whole universe. I felt myself carried up. I heard a door shut and then I was being lowered down, down, but I never reached the bottom of the chasm into which I was being lowered. Everything was peaceful and dark. Sometimes I thought I was a small body, bandaged and swollen, lying on the floor. And sometimes the door would open, sending in a shaft of light. At one time a tall lanky man would enter and briefly stand over this body. At other times, a shorter heftier man would sit by this body and run his hand across the bandaged face below him. Sometimes the hand would part the lips of the still face and a teaspoon would be pushed in and out. The spoon has very thin milk in it. At other times a woman comes in, always silent, and always turns the body this side, and that, now on its back, now on its side. Other faces enter but I don't seem to have enough affinity with them to want to know what their names are and what they want with my body.

But the most memorable and the most outstanding thing I am very aware of whenever I look at the bandaged body that I own and which I can't decide whether to leave altogether or go back to it and assist it to heal, is the face of a small boy that always sits by my body. His eyes are always moist and he's always looking down at my bandaged face. I hear him cry, 'You must not leave me here my friend.' At such times we always seem to leave my body. And we always end up in a wide river on a warm rock overlooking a very wide pool whose depth is immeasurable. Then he says, 'Look there! Look closely! That's where it is.'

Then I remember my body and go back to sit near it, and find that the boy of five years is still sitting there. And the last thing I remember before the peaceful darkness falls on me is the boy saying, 'You must help me to help them when we are grown up.'

And I don't know who 'they' are supposed to be.

Six

I remained unconscious for a whole week, within which time, much happened to change the course of events around both my home and the school.

The first things I saw were two faces which seemed to come from endless space far, far away, battling the thick mist that gradually thinned out so that they became clear before me. Great was my astonishment when on opening my eyes I saw our headmaster's face! At first I was seized with the fear that I hadn't done my homework and must surely be punished and that Kyanzo would be called to do that office. I tried to bolt out of bed, but could hardly lift my body for I was still very weak.

Headmaster Mathayo gently laid me down, passed his hand over my face and asked me how I felt. But my mind was in such a chaotic state that I mumbled something and then changed to all the topics that concerned him. As Hamad later told me with great amusement, I begged the headmaster not to cane me, that I would be a good pupil from then henceforth, that Rural Science was the best house of correction, that Reverend Wranglem was a cheat and an imposter; that I thought Headmaster Mathayo was a kind man but a great fool to beat us—that dances were illegal and the guitar was legal; that rain was the best school rule, and that Kyanzo was the best Protestant manual ever and the headmaster was a great fool and a Christian hypocrite not to follow his example . . . cruel, cruel . . . oh cruel! According to Hamad, here I burst into tears and fought the blanket with such fury that he wondered where the strength had come from. But the headmaster and Hamad (who bore the second face) tried to calm me down, and by the time they managed to, they were fully convinced there was not a worse and a more troublesome imp the world over.

Presently, the trembling and spasms of my body died down and I fell into deep sleep. From that day on, I began to recover and, on the orders of the nurse from the Mission Station, I was to stay in bed and do very little for the next two weeks. In those two weeks the big house became a regular hospital ward. In those two weeks I was so much the centre of attraction and received so many visitors that I began to have a very high opinion of myself. Once my father and mother came. I remember my father sitting on a wooden chair beside my bed and, upon my narration of what had happened, a narration which ended with a burst of tears, my father sat there and said that Mr. Kyanzo was his greatest friend and if he had given me a little more punishment than my body could take, it was solely out of his deep hatred for young men falling into evil. Thus Kyanzo had done it for my good and in accordance with the law that he who denies his son the rod, hates him. This my father said by way of consolation. My mother stood a little behind him, thin as ever, and because of the way my parents looked as they stood before me, I thought that my father would have no second thoughts before he repeated Kyanzo's exploits, using my mother as a stick. At length my father asked me whether I felt I would be strong enough to come home for the holidays, for the others were eager to see me. Despite my burning desire to see my brother, I said 'No!' And from that moment until they left, I just lay on my bed and listened to my father eulogizing upon the subject of sickness, of all the afflicted men and women, of old people of great spiritual strength who found salvation in spirit and tolerance of forgiveness, and of the Great Man of Galilee who voluntarily went to the tree and lost his life that I might be forgiven. Lying on that bed I wondered about this Man, and if he had allowed other men to maul His body the way Kyanzo did mine he would still find enough courage to forgive them, for they *knew* what they did. Kyanzo and the uplifted stick passed before me and if that image had knelt before me a thousand times and begged forgiveness, I knew I would not forgive. For he certainly knew what he did.

My mother said nothing. And I knew she thought it were better she didn't. But as they left, she opened her basket and gave me a bunch of ripe bananas. I thought that that gesture said more to me at that time than all the sermons on earth.

Among the other visitors were my school mates

among whom (of all the people I least expected) was Gruff! And he was not Gruff now. Far from it! For a whole Saturday afternoon, he sat upon the same chair as my father had sat and told the wildest stories I've ever heard. They all had to do with violence and conquest: how a young he-goat had had one of his sprouting horns torn off but had continued the battle with the other horn until the offending battering ram was vanquished; how, when Gruff was my size and age he had beaten every foe in the market-place . . . and how he had seen me vanquish that foe on my first day of arrival in Kyambe and—how on earth could I let a mere wisp of a cough get me down? And, laughing, he said he knew I was a little hypocrite and that I should decide to get up and be about in the next two days. If he found me still wallowing in bed and moaning . . . mmh! He left, and I heard his motor cycle roar down the path as if it dragged my illness away. True to this angry youth's postulates, I was up in two days and when, true to his word, he came on the third day, he found me under the eaves of the old house, basking in the evening sun and attempting to play the guitar. He gave me a pat on the shoulder that nearly sent me sprawling, and said that I was a real man. Which, in fact I felt I was! In the war with illness I felt myself a heroic conquering warrior.

Gruff and Hamad had established a great friendship for each other and I wondered much about this. They seemed to like the same things, do the same things and walk the same way. They would walk together down to the garden, carrying their hoes in their hands and laughing. I would see them, digging side by side and hear their bursts of laughter on these occasions and marvel at this hard-working son of our Chief. These occasions were mainly at weekends, and quite often after school. During the first three days of his digging, Gruff developed ugly blisters which he seemed to be as proud of as any vain woman was of her beauty spots. He would nonchalantly throw down the hoe and parade both hands before me and ask, 'Did you ever have blisters as big as these?' as if to challenge me to get well quickly and acquire some to compete with his.

I wondered very much about the change in Gruff until I found out the reason in the second week of my convalescence—and in the first week of our school holidays. The day was a Thursday and Gruff had come unusually early. Hardly had the Mission bell tolled the third time to announce nine o'clock, than Gruff's motorcycle roared into our compound. Today, he was unusually well dressed. He wore long grey trousers, a white shirt and a tie. Around his neck was a black string which crossed his left breast and fell into his shirt pocket like a police lanyard. He revved his motorcycle and roared it so many times before he switched off the engine, that everybody came out of the house. Hamad was there, dressed in his best clothes. Little Kyanzo was there, also neatly dressed. Eileen came out last and was dressed in a long flowing blue cloth which reached below her knees. In her hand she carried three baskets of different sizes all carefully fitted one inside the other, like the layers of an onion.

When he saw her, Gruff straightened up and breezed out a very airy and charming 'Good morning' to everyone. We chorused good morning and Hamad shook hands with him. Looking straight at Eileen, Gruff flipped up the lanyard with a dexterous flick of the left thumb. And out of his shirt-pocket and bound fast to the lanyard, popped a large watch. He looked at the watch, eyes askance as if it couldn't withstand full human scrutiny, then he said in English, 'Dead on time!'

Except myself, nobody understood him. Then he bowed to Eileen the way his father the chief had bowed to the District Commissioner in the last baraza and said in both English and Vernacular, 'Madam, I have come to help you!'

All of us were dumbfounded and I began to be apprehensive that my hostess was in grave danger and that only Gruff, being a chief's son could help. My mind raced fast across the possibility that Hamad had threatened her life in expiation for her husband's cruelty to myself. Then Gruff said, 'It's a fine market day.'

Eileen said yes it *was* a fine market day but she did not need any help. As Gruff could see, Hamad and her son had made ready to accompany her to market. She thanked him, however, and promised that when Hamad, or I or her son were too busy to help, she would send me to solicit his aid. But Gruff, seeming to think that his father, motorcycle, watch and a police lanyard, should not be let down and that she had no right to refuse his aid, pressed her to comply. Hamad then reminded him that because all three were going to market together as they were engaged upon common business, it wouldn't be easy to take them all upon his motorcycle.

Gruff would *not* be let down and he said that it was not proper that she, a lady, should walk. He would take her on his bike and they would find her ahead at the market place.

'But I want to go with them!' Eileen said, her body trembling as if it knew better what to say and the mouth had let it down. But Gruff did not heed her.

He kept pestering her about the need to be a civilised woman.

At length Hamad got tired of what he called the silliness of a badly brought-up boy, and ordered him to take his 'thing' and ride for ever away from that house. Feeling badly let down, Gruff toyed with the lanyard like a man who thought that all the policemen at his disposal would surely be called to force obedience upon these people. And he stood there, an ugly leer playing upon the corners of his mouth. Then he burst out laughing derisively.

'Do you *know* something my friend? All my life I have never imagined myself talking to a person like you,' he said, looking at his own bright clothes, lanyard and all, as if he called them to witness that such dialogue was far beneath his dignity. Hamad said nothing, but smiled instead; which action badly infuriated the son of our chief.

'My father has always had servants,' pursued Gruff, 'and none of them has ever spoken *one* word to me, let alone argued with me!'

'Look, my friend,' said Hamad, laying his palm calmly upon Gruff's shoulder, 'we don't have much time . . .'

'Keep your dirty hands off me you low-born servant!' Gruff snarled, retreating a step backwards, both arms outstretched before him as if avoiding a leper.

That did it! I saw Hamad stiffen and then in fury, stride to where the motorcycle stood and with his bare hands lift it high above his head. Round and round he whirled it above his head, giving out a throaty sound of anger, like that of a wounded wildcat.

'No. Don't!'

It was Eileen's voice, shrill, sharp and final. And on hearing it, Hamad stopped in midtrack and lowering the motorcycle to his knees, he said, 'Take it!'

Now Gruff moved fast and taking the motorcycle by the seat and handlebars, tottered under its weight and would have collapsed under it, had Hamad not steadied it. Hamad now moved to the side of the house and leaned against it—trembling with the mixture of emotions that welled up in him.

'Get away from here boy, and let me never see you again,' he said in a voice barely above a whisper. Gruff, throwing tantrums like a child of two, wheeled his motorcycle with a great show of pomp and shot out of our compound. I watched him disappear over the hillock, his cycle bumping angrily upon the path and I knew that from then henceforth, that letdown son of a chief would not look at me at school without thinking that he was a weakling who had beeen badly humiliated before a woman, and that I was the only person who knew it.

Like me, Hamad was looking at the disappearing rider and as the latter got out of sight, I heard Hamad say to himself, 'Low-born Servant!'

His head was bowed and looking at him I couldn't believe that he was the same man who had whirled the motorcycle above his head. All his strength seemed to have gone with the rider. I saw Eileen looking at him then, the way women look at their small babies. There was a smile upon that face, mixed with wonder, admiration, respect and it seemed to me that she wanted to tell him something. But when she opened her mouth, all she said was, 'Let's go. We shall be late.'

Obediently, Hamad followed her and with the son at his heels, they were off to market. As they went up over the hillock they made a striking contrast with the rider who went before them—a tightly knit little band of people who seemed to be moving upon a single leg, like a walking mushroom.

When they were gone, an extraordinary atmosphere of silence descended upon my surroundings. It was as if the very earth that was wet with the rains, the gnats that flew from it and back into it, the air that enveloped it and the birds that flew above it and silently fed upon the little gnats—all these were trying to say something. But, like the woman that was my hostess, they knew not how to say it. All was quiet and in that silence I began to wonder about Kyanzo and where he was, and about the builders whose knocking and hammering and laughter had done so much to dispel the gloom of silence.

Feeling bored, I rose and slowly zigzagged down the path to the garden, enjoying the green hue that covered the land. I came upon the garden, at the centre of which there was a huge mango tree. From the tree one could see a much wider area than from the house. From here I traced the river below me as it cut and wound all the way to the plains at the foot of the southernmost hills. I thought about this river and wondered whether it was the same one down which Hamad had swum. And for the rest of that day, I sat under that tree and tried to imagine what his future would be. He worked tirelessly and earned nothing. His livelihood and well-being, even his very life itself, lay in the hands of a man that could as easily dispense with it as a boy would his playthings. I wished I could help him, but all the chances my child's mind could hatch, seemed thoroughly sealed. I tried to imagine him, an old man of seventy, surrounded by many grandsons and wondered what he would tell them, whether he would tell them the story of his life in the days of old when he was powerful and could whirl a motorcycle above his head. Would he talk about me and the lessons I had taught him? I tried hard to see a clear picture of these things. But however much I tried to place him in that distant future, his figure always evaded me. And in the still silence of the surroundings, I seemed to hear a faint echo of a voice which insisted that such a time would never, never come.

They arrived just before the sunset, an occasion I was made aware of by the sudden shrill laughter of little Kyanzo who walked slightly ahead of the others, wielding a new panga they had bought. A short distance behind him, Eileen and Hamad were engaged in conversation as they came home. On his head Hamad had the big basket that was full and bulging, and as he balanced it with his left hand, I was reminded of the story of Atlas, the god who was supposed to keep the world afloat upon his shoulders. Eileen walked slightly in front of him, and had the two baskets placed one upon the other and strapped on to her back. It was an altogether contented party that unloaded themselves in the house and for the first time since I had known her, I heard Eileen hum to herself as she assembled and washed the pots in her preparations for supper.

We ate early and retired to bed, for they were very tired, especially the little boy. When we had closed the door of the big house behind us, Hamad took his guitar and began to play. I lay on my bed of dry banana leaves and sheets, listening to him.

'Won't he get angry?' I asked

'Who?'

'Kyanzo! He said you must never play.'

'Ah yes, but you see, he is not here.'

'Where is he?'

'Don't you know? Ah, but then you wouldn't.'

And he told me about Kyanzo in those days when I was unconscious.

Three days after my punishment, when he had explained to the headmaster about the reason for the severe measures he had taken against me (not failing to say he had done it with a view to making me a better and more obedient pupil according to the disciplinary traditions of Kyambe), the nurse from the Mission Station came to see me and certified that, with proper medication, I would not die. I had no broken bones. My structure was intact except for bad cuts and bruises, one across the face, another on my skull and a nasty bruise across the left side of my breast. Upon Kyanzo's insistence, she had promised to visit me every other day. It was then that Kyanzo decided to use my illness as a reason for getting rid of the builders, whom he had complained about as being lazy and wasting both time and his money. On the afternoon of the fourth day, he had called them and thanked them for their excellent work. No people could have done as much in as little time and it grieved his heart to tell them the heavy news that burdened him. They had to go! There had been an unfortunate incident, the result of which was the little patient, who now shared with them the very house they were building. He was under strict medical orders to keep the surroundings very quiet. So the builders had to leave. For the time being, he would pay them their dues, in case they needed money during these forced holidays. But when I had got better and the doctor's ban on noise had been lifted, and when he had come back from the business trip he was about to embark upon, he would surely contact them so that they might complete the work.

Sadly, the builders had left. As they told Hamad, they were not sad because they were leaving a half-built house as much as the fact that they were parting with our company, which they had grown to like very much. The following day Kyanzo had left, but not before giving Eileen strict orders concerning her conduct, and the son's conduct with regard to Hamad and myself. A servant and a guest never equalled the master and host. No more petty games. She was to observe tough discipline both in her mortal, moral, and spiritual conduct, the latter of which was to be placed under Reverend Wranglem's surveillance on every Thursday (which was our prayer day) and every Sunday. On those days the commandment 'Flee from among them' would be fortified and made more real. And as he told me this, Hamad wondered whom it was that Eileen and little Kyanzo had to flee from, and who were these particular villains that had so much power as to require the combined forces of Reverend Wranglem and the culprit before the culprits were free.

Kyanzo had not indicated when he would be back and Hamad said they expected him any day the following week, for which reason the mother and child were kept in perpetual suspense and conducted themselves very carefully.

Outside the moonlight bathed the earth and streamed through the ventilation spaces of our big house. Through the same spaces, the breeze constantly whispered, cooling my face and wafting away the terrible memories of the weeks gone by. In this coldness Hamad's music rose and fell, like the gentle waves of the sea and I thought it a very peaceful night. As I slept, I felt a strange urge to say a prayer of thanksgiving. But I did not say it. Out of the multitudes of things that constituted this peace, I could not single anything out to be thankful for. And as I finally closed my eyes before the last flickers of the tin-candle, my mouth kept working, over and over, and as Hamad later said, the words I repeated were, 'Thank you.'

I gained strength sooner than I expected for which I will always thank and love both Hamad, Eileen and little Kyanzo. The last was a constant source of diversion for me. On many a morning or afternoon, when Hamad and Eileen went out to work, this little friend, feeling that I must not be left to myself even for a moment, would seek me out and pester me to such a degree that I had to open my mouth and communicate. One afternoon, when I was absorbed in reading a simplified version of Gullivers' voyage to Lilliput, little Kyanzo sat on a stone beside me and asked what I was reading. I said I was reading the story of a big man who found himself among little people.

The boy listened to my story with the greatest attention I had ever seen upon a human face. At the end he asked, 'And did the big man beat the little people?'

'No.'

'Why?'

'He did not need to.'

'But . . . but . . . my father beats me, and mother . . . And he beat you because we are smaller.'

'I don't think so.'

'Why then?'

I didn't know the answer. So I simply reiterated the fact that it was not so.

'Because we did wrong?' he pursued.

'Yes!' I said, relieved.

'But mother does not do wrong. Why then is she beaten?'

I did not know either. But I made a try and said that sometimes people were beaten so that they can become better and be obedient.

'And if they are already obedient?'

'Keeps them more obedient.'

'But they *were* obedient!' he insisted.

'Still, you don't know when they will not be obedient.'

'Why should you beat them if they have not yet been disobedient and if you don't even know whether they will be disobedient?'

I was dumb! I began to fear this little child of five who asked adult questions. And henceforth I did not look at him without feeling that he was going to ask me another adult question before Eileen and Hamad and expose me as a learned book-scholar who knew next to nothing. But he didn't, and for most of the time that I knew him before I left Kyambe Primary, he was a simple little friend, who would not rest until I laughed.

He was growing fatter now, the eyes began to recede, and the chin lost its arrowhead tip. Within the four months that followed, he became a hefty, energetic boy who sang up and down the bench terraces and harassed the garden with impunity. Many an evening he would turn up all by himself, his mouth a thorough mess of ripe mango, raw cassava, wild berries, ripe bananas, tomatoes and pomegranates. And on many evenings Eileen would strip him and plunge him into the warm basin of water, slapping him lightly to which punishments he responded with laughter and glee.

116

Seven

A change was coming over Eileen.

During our holidays, and when I was strong enough to work outdoors, I would accompany both Eileen and Hamad to the young forest which Kyanzo had commanded Hamad to clear. It was then that I began to notice this change. Hamad usually went ahead of us, clearing the shrubs with single swipes of his panga from right and left, like a great warrior that had drunk full with blood and mowed down the enemy right and left, with his sword, unaware of the many spears that were being thrown at him and the noise of battle all round. Eileen would come behind him, collecting the shrubs and heaping them in neat piles for burning. She was always either behind or beside him, either tidying up the ground behind him or, armed with her own panga, she would work beside him with great dexterity and strength. At one time her headgear would be caught in the shrubs as she bent to cut their base, and she would stop to tie it around her middle. And at such times I wondered what Reverend Wranglem would say if he saw her, or whether she was aware of the strict commandment he had always emphasized that: A woman must hide her hair from the sight of the Lord. At first I thought she worked with such determination to show that she was better than her own servant. But as the days passed and the work progressed, it dawned on me that she loved this work. She loved swinging her arms right and left. She loved to see the dense shrubs obey

her will and fall away. She would plunge her left foot
into the dark area ahead of her. Then, using her left
arm, she would bend over a full cluster of shrubs in
one sweeping motion. Then she would cut their
turgid stems close to the wet earth, with the panga in
her right hand. Then using the panga she would flick
the stems up, snatch them in her now free left hand
and wrench the whole cluster from the rest of the
shrubs.

Sweat and dry leaves would fall down her face. She
would wipe them with the palm of her hand. Her
small tight-lipped mouth would smile with satisfaction as she got back to work. Looking at her, I could
not believe that she was the same apathetic being that
came out of the storm, curled up like a cabbage. In
the short time I had seen this woman, I realised that
she liked the work that was free, where she was her
own law-maker and where she was free to compete
with any impediment for mastery over the soil. As
she won that battle and helped Hamad free the soil of
those shrubs, I thought that that freedom glowed
within her too. She was much more talkative now and
cracked innumerable jokes. Once she taunted me and
asked me if I thought I was a good scholar? I said I
believed I would be. Then she asked me, 'Scholar-
that-is-to-be. Tell me; when will they ever teach you
how to work upon the land—how to use the panga
and the hoe?'

I replied that I would learn that art by and by,
although I knew a little of it and I hoped that there
was a lot of that intelligence high up in the academic
tree.

Then she said, 'It's a false hope, scholar. Those
white people are all scholars like you. Yet they know
very little about basic things. We women take care

of their children. Our men take care of their land and their work. And all they do is drive their cars and gossip. If all your learning comes from them, how will you ever learn to till the land? Tell me; do they ever teach you anything about work with your hands.'

I confidently said they did.

'And what do you learn, if you can't wield a panga?'

'Well, writing—I mean *good* handwriting. Good drawing of maps . . .'

'Maps? What are they?'

I was in my stride! I explained all, however little, I knew about geography and the drawing of maps, the representation of lands on paper; pairs of compasses, pairs of dividers, pencils, rubbers, rulers, scales and ink!

'Ink? . . .' she asked.

I said of course! She surely must know it! The stuff we write with. And in geography ink was very valuable. It was water on paper. And it was always blue, because water was blue.

Eileen laughed outright. And, from the corner of my eye I saw Hamad laughing mischievously and wagging his forefinger at me. Then Eileen took my hand and led me to the stream beside our house and said, 'Look there! What do you see?'

'Water,' I said.

'What colour is it?'

'Well, it's muddy.'

'Like my clothes, isn't it?'

'Yes.'

Then she dragged me to the centre of the clearing where we kept our fresh water in a gourd. Then she poured into a ladle and asked me, 'What's this?'

'Water! agh!'

'What colour is it?'

'Aigh! No colour!'

'Didn't *you* say that your water is always blue?'

'Well . . .' I began. But before I had finished, her mind had already summed me up as an academic liar and she said, 'Do we pay for your schooling that you may come home and tell us lies? . . . And what *do* you do besides ink?'

I said that sometimes the teacher took us out and showed all the land around us.

'And then?'

Curse this bothersome woman!

'Well'—I said . . . 'we went back inside, wrote what we had seen, and the lesson was over.'

'And now you know about the land, and rivers and everything?' I replied that it was so.

'They never teach you why you must learn about the land?'

'No!'

'Nor how to get out, work upon it and plant, care for it and get a harvest?'

—'Well . . . not yet.'

'I'm not surprised then that you can't work properly. I can forgive a small child working like a snail and making a thorough mess of it. But a young man and an educated one at that . . . not even knowing how to cut a shrub! When my son Kieni (little Kyanzo) goes to school shall I pay school fees to have him sit beside buildings like the white man, watch me work, go back inside and just write what he has seen? What kind of lazy education is that?'

'Well . . . er . . .,' I began.

'Useless!' Eileen stormed. 'Waste of money, waste of good people! If you can't learn to do anything with it, it has absolutely no use. Little Scholar, learn to do things with all those explanations of yours.'

After that she bent down and whacked those shrubs with such vigour and speedy success, that I felt ashamed and blamed our teacher for not instructing us on this art in Rural Science. That night I lay down staring up at the streams of moonlight and wondered why we had never been told why water was always blue on paper, and how I would distinguish a river that was muddy from one that was clear.

When we had cleared the shrubs and Eileen had heaped them neatly at the side, we now embarked upon the trees. We would each cut down a tree and then cut it up in small pieces for firewood, which we heaped before our house. The twigs, we heaped among the shrubs so that the place intended for the garden was clean. After this, Hamad took his hoe and dug out all the stumps. It was a pleasure to see him work and hear his hoe, whistling through the air and crack into some root. And during these times, she would always be there, cleaning up the large clearing. At times, when there was not much to do, she would stand and look at Hamad as he wielded his hoe. The expression on her face at these times was hard for me to describe. It was not a full smile that I saw upon her face, nor sadness, nor joy. It was something between all these, as if the breeze was too strong upon her face and was bent on dispelling any emotion that was registered there. But I noticed that by and by, her eyes had lost that brownish film of many days before. They had even lost the perpetual watery shine which had stood there as she fed me in my early days of weakness. Now they were clear and bright and alert so that, like Hamad, she seemed to see through my head with those dark eyes. When that happened I always felt as if the two of them had conspired to worm out any traces of lies within my head whether academic or mundane.

All this time Hamad would work on, unaware of the eyes that traced every fibre of his shoulder muscles and every movement of his hoe. He would look up once, suddenly, as if a thousand voices called out to him from behind the hill across the river and then he would see her. In those rare times I would see a smile flash across his face. It was the kind of smile I usually saw on the faces of small children, rising abruptly from within, bursting across the whole face with such force it made the eyes half shut and linger there, bright as the noonday sun untainted by sunset. I noticed that when their eyes met and after Hamad's smiles, they would quickly look down to their work as if some unseen authority had pointed his staff at them and singled them out for punishment for an evil I could not understand. But to me that saw them, Hamad's smile seemed to linger on in the air around them and Eileen's intense look seemed for ever to cut a path across the air between them. Long afterwards, when the land had been cleared, that smile and look seemed to stay; and when the neighbour's bulls had been hired and the whole clearing had been ploughed, the look and the smile seemed to hover around the deep, dark brown soil. That look and that smile were there when Hamad went before her, digging little holes with his hoe in straight lines. They were there when Eileen came three steps behind him, throwing the grains into the holes and covering them. They were there when the seeds sprouted, when the young plants fluttered happily in the breeze. They hovered above the new garden and among the strong maize plants whose tassels seemed to sing to one another and to the weaver birds that settled among

122

the tassels and sang incessantly to one another. In short, that innocent smile and look seemed to spread a boundless agreement with all that lived, and the agreement itself took all life in its fold with one emphatic—Yes!

As the days went by, I noticed that both Hamad and Eileen were gradually becoming like little children, a thing which made little Kieni burst out in delight, but which disconcerted me immensely. At home I would watch Hamad play a football game with Kieni, unmindful of my dark looks of recrimination. They would use anything for the ball, from ripe sodom apples to young oranges and even pebbles! But I would be delighted to see Hamad's look of concern as he bound Kieni's toe, whenever he had hurt it during those games. They had innumerable games in their store, including hide and seek, where they used the forest with unbounded zeal, marksmanship, making faces, making noises, athletics, high jump . . . In short, these two males seemed to develop incredible ingenuity for making a game out of anything within sight. Once little Kieni stubbed his toe and began to cry. I was expecting Hamad to bend down and bind that toe. But he did nothing. He just stood, arms across his chest, looking down at the weeping boy, his head inclined to one side. Over his face was spread the most comic picture of grief I ever did see. When the boy looked up and saw Hamad's face, he burst out laughing. It was only then that Hamad bent down and bound that toe.

Often I would join in their games, hesitant at first, until, as the dark sobriety of school lessened within my mind, I began to be less hesitant about movement and joined their games with the enthusiasm of any young goat alive.

During these games, Eileen sat under the eaves and watched us. But as the fun became more intense, she began to join us, and a better player I never saw. Often we would team up in twos and engage in the most furious contest imaginable. But it was in football of all games, that Eileen excelled, at which times I always insisted that she be my team mate so that we should win. When the game started, she would jump at that ball with fury, her fists raised above her shoulders, her legs flying all over the place until Hamad's own dextrous ones were quite defeated. She would pursue that ball right into the thickets. For we had not defined our boundaries except by the goal stones. It was allowed to bypass the goal or overshoot it and still continue the game and score from behind! And I would watch Eileen play the ball into the thickets, her feet working this way and that like a regular matchet, and she would pursue that ball until she made sure our side won. Mostly we won. At other times it was adults against the small ones and Kieni and I would arm ourselves with courage and make sure we came to at least a draw, even if our opponents were the most formidable players upon earth. Sometimes, when we were in danger of losing, I would detect an element of pretence in our opponents, who would let us win, much to my disappointment, but much to Kieni's delight who would prance about and shout, 'We won, yahaa—we won!'

These games had no referees and it depended upon the honesty of each one of us to keep the game clean. At one time Hamad fell and accidentally touched the ball in a football game. When he got up he stood rooted on the spot, his right hand raised up to the skies. The others continued with the game until we discovered that Hamad was no longer playing. Asked

124

by Eileen what ailed him and why his hand was up in the air like a railway signal for 'all clear', Hamad admitted that he had handled the ball and the game could not continue! Upon which we went back to where he had transgressed, a penalty on his side was awarded unanimously, and the game continued.

In the evenings and after supper, we sat outdoors when there was moonlight. In the cool silence of the evening, Hamad would play his guitar and we would sing to its music. As the days passed I would play too and they would join me. Then I would feel elated and inspired and would play that guitar like one possessed. One evening, when it was clear, and the moon bathed the earth with unusual brightness and when it was quiet upon the whole brooding land and across the sky above where the myriad bright stars twinkled, we sat outdoors again, listening to Hamad playing his guitar. At first he played the songs we had sung hitherto, and clapped. Then he sang another Swahili song:

> Blessing Blessing
> Blessing upon the land
> All the journeys end
> In blessing upon the land
> And we shall try to be able
> And we shall try to be able.

He sang alone, on and on, his eyes shut, looking up at the depths of the sky. Then, as the words faded away—'and we shall try to be able'—the guitar wailed again in the solo and involuntarily I held my breath. He had begun to play the sad song I had heard him play before the builders. He played on, his emotion intensifying with the intricate cry of the solo. Then he began to sing in a high tenor voice, and in that

125

language I did not understand. He seemed more possessed by that song than he had ever been before. At one line in the refrain he broke out in Swahili and the words rippled up the six strings of that guitar and asked, 'Why did she have to die?'

The words were threaded into his whole being and were cried off to the sky into which he gazed with his now watery eyes, so that I was forced to look up there expecting to find someone who would answer the question, 'Why did she have to die?' But there was no one there and the sky was silent and brooding in the moonlight as before, and the stars twinkled up there, and in their false light that they'd never bequeath to anyone here on earth, I seemed to sense an answer that no one could or would give until the stars lay behind mortal man.

When I withdrew my eyes, I found Hamad's still peering into the sky as if he disagreed with me that there was no answer there. Eileen's hand was drawn into his right one so that the back of it lay flat against the strings and over the round opening into the guitar's resounding box. Gradually, she moved closer and sat against him, looking at the moonbathed landscape before her as if she too contradicted me that there was no answer anywhere upon that land.

They sat quietly, unmoving, each seeming lost in thought. I could not withdraw the guitar from Hamad's lap, so I just sat doing nothing, feeling an uneasy guilt of what I didn't know or couldn't define. Kieni had long gone to sleep across his mother's lap and I seemed to be the only one awake, alone, outside the triangle. Silently, I stole back to my bed and lay upon it. For a long time I stared at the brightened roof and thought about the song, and its woman that had to die. The image of Hamad holding a small girl in his arms, all alone on a colonial farm, flashed across my mind, and in the memory of that song and that one line, I too, asked the question. I too, could not find the real answer to the riddle of this stupidity that for a few minutes of forced labour that girl had to die. I lay upon my bed and could not sleep. Long after Hamad had lain upon his, where he seemed to be less disturbed now than I was, I thought about this riddle and at length I asked, 'Hamad?'

'Yes.'

'Can't you forget her? She is dead, she can't come back, you could do nothing beyond what you did to save her.'

'No,' he blurted out. 'I did nothing—I could do nothing! I stood on that bridge and watched her die.'

'But I thought the girl at the farm . . .'

I could not and did not finish. Instinctively I felt this was unjust, twisting the knife in his wound. He was silent for a long time. Gradually, the moon had set, leaving us in the darkness. Out of that darkness came Hamad's voice, low at first.

'No. It was not the girl at the farm. It was . . . my family . . . my mother.'

He did not ask whether I was asleep or awake and listening. He just poured his story out into the darkness. And in the silence of those dark early hours of the morning, his voice rose and fell with his story:

'It was long ago. I was about the age of Kieni, Eileen's son. We lived together my mother, my sister and I—the three of us, near the sea-shore. My father died before I was born. He was a fisherman. One day he went far out to sea in his boat, and he never returned. People say that on that day the fishermen saw him paddle out . . . out to sea . . . as if he was following a prize fish he had to catch. He reached the

127

reefs where the sea is always raging. Then they saw him disappear, and neither he nor his boat were ever seen again. I never knew him.

'Soon after, my uncle advised my mother to take my sister and me and move further into the interior, where the clan owned land, on either side of the big river. We migrated inland and, with the help of the men and women of our clan, my mother built a hut on the little hill overlooking the river. I used to sit before the hut and look at that river below me— always flowing, silently meandering across the plains on its way to the sea, near where my home used to be. Sometimes it would be clear. Then all of a sudden it would be muddy and swell to break its banks. We lived here for some time in peace, and I grew up. It was here that I first became aware of the world, the people around us, and the cattle, sheep, and the goats we kept.

About this time, there was a rumour that a white man, who always wore a white helmet, had camped about three ridges north of our clan-land. Nobody bothered about him at first. There was enough land for everyone and the stranger said he did not need much anyway. Just a little plot to build himself a small house. He began to mix with the people in the market place. He was a very poor man. Always in the same clothing, the same boots. He could not buy much from our market, but he always rode out of it a happy man, his horse laden with food and fruits that the women had given him as gifts. They liked to tease him and wondered whether he had a woman and, if so, why she never came to market as other women did.

'About a year later, another white man came into the market place, accompanied by a group of askaris. I went to that meeting at the market place where, through an interpreter, the white man said he was a representative of his government and that his government had ordered him to tell us that the land which we had settled and cultivated was no longer ours and that it had been set aside for European settlement. We must evacuate it. He gave us a month in which to do so. Then he left.

'People thought that it was a mere joke, just as they made a joke of the lone poor man who never missed a market day. Then one day in the evening the askaris stormed upon us, clearing everyone away from their homes. Except for two or three, these men were not from our area and did not even heed the cried of the women and children. Instead, they swept through the villages, beating the men and raping the women and burning our homes. And all this time they laughed as if it was a game . . .

' . . . People were running! My mother took my hand and ran down the hill, following my elder sister who ran ahead to catch up with the rest of the fleeing people at the wooden bridge. Behind us, the askaris came running, their boots sounding like a herd of many horses. Behind them, and rallying them, was the white man. Whips cracked and, in terror, we ran on. Then we came upon the river . . .

'The bridge was upstream to our left, and my sister was running faster to catch up with the bunch of women and children fleeing across it. There was a lot of noise, mad laughter and the crack of the whips behind us, and before us, men, women, and children in a panic—weeping, shouting . . . running. My sister had reached the bridge and . . . slipped . . . into the river. No one helped her. Everyone was running. It was as if madness had descended upon everyone.'

129

Hamad was silent then, barely audibly, 'My sister fell into the river and nobody helped her. Nobody. Then my mother let go of my hand and, she was running, pushing the women and children aside. I saw her standing on the bridge in that white cloth she always wore, golden in the setting sun. Many voices called her to stop. Many hands tried to withhold her. But she wrestled like one possessed, calling, "My daughter! My daughter!" '

'She jumped into the river . . .'

Hamad was sobbing now, like a little child, and in between sobs he said . . .

'She knew there were crocodiles there. She knew it and jumped into the river! I reached the bridge and stood there, looking at the turmoil in the dark water below. The white man and askari passed by, chasing our people. But I did not hear them. I did not see them. The water below was frothing . . . foam, waves, shapes . . . shapes . . . shapes. Then in a flash, I saw my mother's upper body bolt out of the boiling water, facing the bridge above her. She lifted her hand then, as if she sought my help. That was the last I saw of her before a force dragged her underwater. And I was standing on the bridge, crying. It was getting dark. But no darkness could hide the crimson blood upon the surface of that stagnant water . . .

'I never saw my sister . . .'

A long silence followed in which only his sobs broke the deep silence of the night.

'My mother and my sister were dead and I was left alone. From that day on, I lived with my uncle up a hill on the other side of the river, overlooking the bridge. Every evening of the days that followed, I went to the bridge. It seemed that they were still with me and I would sit there for a long time, talking to them. Sometimes they would ask me who those people were . . . those people who kept hammering across the river. And I knew they meant our people who worked for the new settler and who were now fencing the land across the river. At times my mother would come to me when I was asleep and ask whether I was eating well and why I grew thin, placing her hand on my face and telling me not to cry. Then she would tell me to be strong and courageous for he can't win. But I didn't know who *he* was. At other times it was my sister, and I would dream that we were playing hide and seek.

'From my uncle's home I used to see the men go to work at the farm across the bridge. It was a long, long, time before I could cross the bridge and work for the same man who robbed me of my mother and sister. But the time came when I had to do something, to work, and get some money. I went into the town and here I peddled water for my master who was an Arab. I would put about six tins of water on to a wagon and go along the streets calling out to customers, selling it. Then I would go back for more.

'At length, I got tired of this routine with its small pay and went back to my uncle. He told me that if I was interested in working as a labourer, the settler across the bridge would employ me. The following morning, I accompanied the men to work. The man who stood before me and enlisted me was the same poor man who used to come to our market, so long ago. And that man was Mnazi Mkavu.'

'Mnazi Mkavu!' I cried.

'The same!'

Hamad was quiet for a long time. Then he turned on his side and pulled the blanket over his head.

The birds were singing when I finally went to sleep.

And I did not wake up until the sun was high in the sky. I went out and stretched, feeling bewildered by the sudden experience of waking up late and long after everyone else. Neither Hamad nor Eileen were about. I walked down to the hut in which I found Kieni busy feeding the fire, so that the pot might be kept boiling. He was humming to himself, which hum was not interrupted either by my intrusion or the large piece of meat that he kept turning and turning inside his mouth, an exercise which played magic tricks upon his brow. He had this trick of pushing the piece of meat right against the side of his cheek, making it look as if a mini-head was about to sprout therefrom. Then, as suddenly, he would transfer the piece to the other cheek which would also look as if it threatened to sprout a headling. And the whole exercise was performed with such absorption and skill and amid such humming that he seemed to be transformed into a merry little creator.

Presently he asked me whether I had breakfasted. I said that I hadn't, so he brought me two boiled eggs and some tea that had gone very cold. All the while he seemed to be bubbling with mirth and when I asked him what occasioned this condition, he turned his head aside, eyed me askance, transferred the now depleted 'headling' to the other cheek, and in the most humble voice imaginable, said that the eggs had actually been three (lifting three fingers) and that he had eaten the third one.. When I enquired about this behaviour which was likely to make him a thief prematurely, he replied that when the sun reached about *here* (indicating horizontally with his palm) and I had not woken up, he had decided to eat the egg—because then I wouldn't need *three* eggs before lunch. By the same computation, he was about to eat the

132

second one and would eat the other one just before his mother returned and served lunch, if I hadn't shown up when I did. I ate silently, wondering at this acute precision of reasoning in which the old proverb about a familiar ghoul not altogether eating up his familiar culprit—was glorified.

After my late breakfast, I ventured outside. Hamad and Eileen were in the newly cleared ground. They worked close together, just as they had done on the day when she upbraided me for lack of geographical application and as they would continue to do so for many days to come. They talked as they worked and this continued to the end of the stretch they were weeding. There was an air of complete unawareness of anything around them except the weeds they up-rooted. I felt I would be an intruder, so I selected a particular weedy area below them and began to culti-vate, and pretended to be absorbed in this area until Eileen decided that lunch was ready. All the time, I watched them. And all the time they talked and laughed together. Sometimes, as they worked, one would unearth something interesting. Only then would their work stop and, together, they would pore over the object, with the absorption and interest matched only by that of little children. And some-times one would accidentally uproot a young maize plant and then bend down to re-plant it with an expression of both regret and gentleness upon the face as if the doer regretted the action and was begging forgiveness of the young plant. At such times, the other would join in and fix attention upon what the other did, like a lawyer defending his business partner in a maize court.

Once Eileen called out to me and asked how the scholar was doing, and whether I didn't think theirs a better occupation than all the books on earth. I was not ashamed then, but now that I have grown much and read much and have become a very monument of facts and theories, I *am* ashamed to say that I agreed with her and forgive myself because I was only a child who could be very easily swayed by the smallest argument.

In the evenings we sat before the fire when there was no moonlight. Hamad's guitar would boom through the whole room and his voice ring beautifully to the music. While we sat and listened, I would occasionally glance at Eileen's face, now fat and round, and every time I looked at it, her dark eyes would be upon the singer, as if she expected to see a figure pop out of the songs in the air, and proclaim itself Hamad's twin. Her little mouth had grown even smaller to give more room to the cheeks that were growing more and more puffed-up as if a swarm of bees stung her afresh at the beginning of each week.

At other times we told stories. This we would do in turns. Each night a total of six stories had to be told. The adults would tell two each and the young ones one each. Should anyone fail to meet the requirements one would borrow from he that had more, on condition that the borrower would perform a desired errand for the lender. By the end of the fourth day, Hamad accumulated such a school of borrowers that he ran out of errands to be performed. The worst borrower was Kieni, who, poor soul, could never go beyond, 'Once upon a time'. He would be word-perfect up to that distinguished point and then roll his eyes in perplexity as if he wondered what particular deity 'Once upon a time' was, and why he had to be addressed before any stories were told. I was next in deficiency. All I knew were two stories taken straight out of Aesop's fables which, after I had narrated with great relish, Hamad stared at me and said he had heard them before. But I didn't have any others in store on account of my strict upbringing, in which folk stories were looked upon as manifestations of the Devil's Wiles. And before the school re-opened and I was intellectually occupied of an evening with homework, I got so heavily in debt that Hamad's clothes shone with constant cleaning. Eileen was second best in this exercise and I was convinced that she could have done better if she had tried. But she seemed to enjoy failing so that Hamad would rescue her. These stories continued well into the night and little Kieni, having proved himself unfit, would quietly slink into his bed, where his snores would punctuate the stories like the voice of the original storyteller come to confirm that, despite the thousands of years, the story remained unchanged. Always the dark eyes of the young woman were upon this storyteller. I gradually began to feel an intruder and became increasingly uneasy; and for a long time afterwards, I wondered why I felt thus.

When at last, we rose to go to bed Hamad would linger, ever so slightly, at the door. Always the dark eyes would meet his as we said good night. Once, when we had said good night, I saw her start from her chair as if it was in danger of falling through the floor, her mouth slightly open. Then we shut the door behind us. After our door of the big house was banged behind us, I heard hers creak open. I lay on my bed and listened to her light steps as she walked to and fro before her house. At one time the footsteps came near to ours and I expected her to knock at the door, but she seemed to think better of it and went back. Long afterwards, I heard her own door creak slowly before she bolted it—with a most unusual fury. Then I knew that she was deeply troubled about this man who would not look at her without drawing out of her the most incredible fidgets I had ever seen.

Eight

One Thursday, in the last week before our school re-opened, they left early together, intending to go to market. Kieni and I were to remain behind, and not stir from the neighbourhood, for visitors might come and find the home deserted. We stood on the verandah, watching them about to disappear behind the hillock. But, just before they completely disappeared, I thought I saw them branch away from the path and cut across the grass up the mountain towards the forests above. To this day, I feel guilty of what I did then and I am even ashamed to own it. But I felt compelled to find out what they were about. Leaving little Kieni under strict orders not to leave the house, lest his mama came and didn't find him at home, I cut straight across the side of the mountain, now plunging into the thick grass, now sliding up and down the banks of various brooks as I madly tore up the mountain, intending not to lose them before they reached the forest.

I reached the edge of the forest without being discovered by anybody, for the grass around this place was about as tall as I was. Under the trees, the forest was clear and without any undergrowth. In places, the rays of the morning sun filtered through the spaces above, illuminating the ground.

There was no trace of them anywhere and, waiting for them to come within sight, I was seized with a debate that didn't seem to be a part of myself and which racked me with restlessness like Ahazuerus, or like the Roman, Pontius Pilate before he washed his hands. The participants were voices and they seemed to emanate from the centre of the forest . . . no, from the very earth itself, clear and to my conscience-stricken mind, audible and at times condemning.

—Why are you here? What are you doing here? What will you gain by eavesdropping? Go back home, Go back home, Go back home!

—Nonsense! I'm on a holy mission. Those adults lied to us. They said they were going to market but they didn't!

—And what if they didn't? What is that to you?

—Everything! It's not right! *Why* did they come to the forest? To hide I am sure! And if it is to hide why *must* they hide? To do evil. And what greater evil can a man and a married woman perform? Eh? Tell me. What evil is this for which the people of God stoned and cast aside the evil-doer? Adultery!

—Adultery? Judge ye that ye be not judged!

—Nonsense. It is my duty to see that evil be not done; that these people tread upon the path of right-eousness.

—Brother's keeper? Brother's keeper? Eh?

—Right! I will be my brother's keeper.

—By what right? Who gave *you* leave to be your brother's keeper? Have you been keeper unto your-self so much, that now you be his keeper?

—Yes! I have been keeper enough. I have not committed it. And I am glad that I have not com-mitted it.

—Yet you would if you could. You want to find out now, that you may feel superior to them; that you may look upon them and say to yourself, 'I know their secret'—and on the day when you yourself also want to commit it, why, you shall come to her and say, 'I know your secret and I will tell!' . . . Look around now, in this forest and find me a beast that will even dream of that lowly action!

—I have *not* committed it. I would not do that. My reasons here are purely moral.

—Moral! Admit it, Kituku. You are here that you may derive pleasure from eavesdropping. Did anyone ever eavesdrop on your mother and father? Would you want anyone to eavesdrop on you?

—No!

—Why?

—It's none of their business!

—That's right, Nor is this any of *your* business. Go home now! To your business—Go home . . . Go home and keep young Kieni company, for he is afraid, all alone beside the forest. Go home now . . .

Thus the argument, thus the triumph. But I could not go home even though I knew what I did was not right. Once I had eavesdropped on the conversation of two young men as they sat on the grass, in the pastures, tending their cattle and sheep. They had been talking about their experiences with various women, how this one just lay like a log; how that one whirled him about like the angry wind of the storm and confounded his senses into oblivion, how her fingers played music upon his back, how it was all very nice and how, among all of them the young men could not distinguish which was which in the darkness for all women were women.

The youths had aired their experiences, and as they

painted all those sweet-and-agonizing pictures, I had felt strange sensations dance up and down my body and concentrate below my navel and make me awake to the fact that there was something there, that it was more undisciplined than either my finger or my toe, that it became an active participant when certain topics were under discussion.

No topic was under discussion now, but images that denoted thousands of similar topics now danced around my head—for which store of knowledge, the grown up youths of Kyambe school should be credited. Standing there, waiting for Hamad and Eileen to reveal themselves, these images had such influence upon my mind that my whole body was in great rebellion against both me and reason, and of its own accord, out-danced both of them. And, true to the moral that a good dancer will dance the way the drums rumble, I danced on the spot, waiting for the new music.

It came. And in the form of a couple who talked and laughed and were unsuspecting of any eavesdropper.

They burst out of the tall grass and into the forest, holding hands. In the other hand, Eileen held blue, red, and white flowers while Hamad's was busy feeding grass stalks into his mouth, where his teeth cut them up and his tongue spat them out with great rapidity.

They did not see me but passed by and sat on a mat of green grass where the rays of the sun penetrated. For a long time, they sat and talked and exchanged so many little tokens that I thought the whole exercise very stupid. Upon which my body let go of its dancing spree and I became normal—certainly more normal I thought, than those mad creatures in that pool of light. Now Hamad was engaged in cutting the long blades of green grass and passing them along to Eileen who made a mat the size of a saucer. She did this quietly with an absorption I had never before seen upon her face. Both faces were calm, very calm and the impression they gave me was that of two young children who had not the slightest care about the world around them. I thought that Eileen was making something of consequence. But when it was finished she threw it gently to Hamad, who threw it back. And they played this game until the green little round disc had become sheer tatters. Then they threw the pieces away and joined hands.

They said very little. Mostly they just looked at one another as if behind the eyes of each one there was a whole world that on-lookers could not comprehend but were very glad that it was there. Tears came down Eileen's cheeks and all the time she was smiling, those white even teeth sparkling in the broad shaft of sunlight and I thought those drops of tears the most beautiful sight indeed. And at the sight of these tears, Hamad would involuntarily pick a petal from the flower and paste it on his right hand small finger and gently trace the tear from the lower eyelid, down to the cheek, until the petal had drunk its fill and broken apart. Then Eileen would make as if to raise her hand, but the gesture would seem to take too much energy and she would put it down.

Thus they remained, for a long time.

'What is your real name?' Hamad asked at length.

'Eileen.'

'No. I mean the one your mother gave you.'

'Mumbua.'

'Mumbua!' Hamad repeated. 'The Daughter of the

140

Rain? A beautiful name on the tongue. Why don't people use it then?'

'I lost it when I married,' Eileen said. 'But let's not talk about that now,' she said, drawing closer to him.

She had her arms around him, drawing him to herself and all the images came from nowhere and whirled around my head, bringing upon me such spasms of drumming and dancing that I feared the music was too loud and that they might discover me. Now she touched his legs and thighs and the drums screamed to a frenzy until, holding that caressing hand as gently as the sea breeze of the morning, Hamad said, 'No.'

She continued.

'No. Remember I am . . . a servant . . .'

'I know that. But you are free now. I set you free a long time ago. That night . . . when you played and sang.'

'Yes Eileen. Still . . . you are a wife and a mother to another man's child. A wife to . . . my . . . master!'

'Wife!' she said hotly, disengaging herself. 'What wife? Is to be beaten, commanded and abused a marriage? I am married by custom and Church. When we stood before the altar he vowed he would love me and care for me till death separated us. But he did not qualify that love, or care. Even a crocodile loves. It loves meat so much, it will even smile at the sight of a man. And it will care to the point of guarding that carcass under and above water. We have been married long, and never once does he look upon me and smile. Not once has he looked upon me as a man should his wife. And I have lived through it all these years. Most of the time he was not even aware that I was there. Always business . . . Will business and money look at me and make me feel . . . feel . . . loved?'

Hamad seemed lost, transfixed. In my imagination, I could almost see the bridge and a woman looking up at him, momentarily before her last struggle for life ended, under that troubled surface. Gradually he became aware of her and now looked at her like a man, alternating between sobbing and laughing. Slowly he pulled her to himself and they lay together on that patch of grass. The shaft of light illuminated them and gradually passed over them and shadows followed it as if to confirm the fact that even life itself, like the light of day, was short. They lay, and did nothing except confound my wicked imagination with shame. For they only lay still in each other's arms, deep in peaceful sleep. And as I crept from my hiding spot, with neither drumming nor music in my body, I thought how untrue were the stories of the senior friends I had at Kyambe that, whenever a man and a woman met in private, sex must abound. I now look upon those days and blame it all on adolescence, for even animals have outgrown such lowly-born thoughts.

Silently, I stole out of that vicinity where peace and quiet reigned and re-entered the grass-covered area. When I reached the edge of the forest, and the clear bright sunlight burst all round me, I started. I felt a chill over my whole body as if the sun had suddenly been drained of its heat by an eclipse, yet by some miracle had maintained its brightness. In the fear of that chill, plus the feeling of guilt and ill thoughts pertaining to that peaceful couple that had called me 'friend' and had respected me, I plunged into that grass and blindly tore down the hill. All the while, the picture of them lying so still, unsuspecting, honest and frank with one another, that picture became a scourging demon, always asking me, 'Why did you do it? Why?' And the earth, maddened by my wild flight would echo, 'I didn't! I didn't do it.' From that day on, I would not look at either of them, and their straight look at one another full of happiness and contentment, without lowering my eyes. I plunged on through the grass, and did not stop until I was within fifteen metres of my home.

A figure stood there, alone, looking in the direction of our school, deep in thought. When it became aware of me, it turned and I gasped. Kyanzo! Kyanzo had come back—and at *this* time!

He did not greet me. His bulging eyes stared at me and I thought he had not slept for many days. With those hostile, staring eyes of his, he took note of every movement I made, every fidget, everything about me was taken down in his memory, and I stood there like a hare caught in the python's hole. I scratched my head and tore some hair out of it. Then I fell to pretending that my nails were too long and had to be cropped, one by one. I sweated. I scratched. I became stiff and cold. And still he stared at me. Then he smiled, the kind of smile that only a fully-knowing and confident winner can afford . . . spider . . . Fly . . . NET!

'My friend . . . come here . . . here . . . come here!' he called, much as any kind master might call a puppy-dog. I edged nearer, apprehensive of this technique—and horrified.

'No. Don't be afraid. I won't beat you now; never again.'

I reached his feet and looked up at him. His gaze travelled to the mountain, up the path I had paved as I ran down the soft and sloping green grassland. Then the unexpected happened. He embraced me so that my head was hidden under his armpits. And in a very clear, cold voice, he asked, 'Where have you been all morning?'

The voice seemed to come from the heavens, levelled at the slope of the mountain whence it bounced back and hit my ears, now a subdued echo.

'Do not lie to me. Tell me everything.' Again the echo! And I was caught in the power of this oracle.

'I went . . . I went up the mountain.'

'What were you doing up there?'

'. . . Looking for the *Mutuo* shrubs! Brooms for school . . .' I lied.

'Which opens in four days' time?'

'Er . . . I had to know where I could find them so that on Sunday I would . . .'

'Don't lie!' he snapped and ground his teeth.

'Well . . . I . . .'

'And where is my child!'

'I left him here!'

'When?'

'A few minutes ago . . . when I went up the mountain.'

He released me and pushed me away from him.

'Kituku, the one thing I can *not* stand is a liar. Sit there . . . And sit still,' he blurted out.

I sat on the grass and listened, with increasing horror eating my whole body.

He had come back a week before! And as he told me this, he waited for the fact to sink in so that I could draw my own conclusions. Then he continued: he had met a friend! Formerly he had hated all chiefs and all their offspring, but now he respected them for they were more intelligent, more observant of morals and more concerned over the moral standard of a community than . . . than . . . *servants*!

He spat the last word as if it was corroding poison.

144

—Servants! the uneducated, the ungodly! Servants, the scum of the earth who knew no morals, who practised no honesty because they never knew what it was. *Servants* that knew no gratitude that knew no ...*respect*!

And in a much quieter tone, almost confidentially, 'Yes, God forgive me! I had thought of chiefs and their sons as the greatest threat to our public well-being; they who serve the very people who torment us, who grant us small tokens of their business. But today I raise them higher than the greatest mountain on earth.' He talked on, as if he didn't care whether I was there.

He related how, coming home a week before, he had met *that son of our chief who went to school with me*, how the son had hinted that something bad might be happening in his family, that perhaps *I* knew it and might help him discover it; how I had always seemed to him to be a confidant, a protector of the evil that was brewing. He went on, in a pained voice and I learned that he had been there, hovering near us, registering every move, every laugh, every spoken word, every joke which his mind had misconstrued. He had known that his wife and Hamad would be going to market early that morning. And he had come. In short, he had known everything, heard everything!

He concluded his story, that the servant had now become the master and that nothing remained.

'Nothing remains,' he said, with his face looking at the floor as had Eileen's on the night he whipped me, I saw it contort and I knew he was fighting hard to keep his tears from falling. He sighed, sniffed and assumed his stolid composure. For the rest of the time, until his son entered, crying and panting,

Kyanzo said not a single word more, and his eyes never left mine. When he embraced his hesitant son and had tickled his side so that the boy laughed and even gathered enough courage to remain by his father's side, he smiled at both of us. His teeth flashed, white, clean and well maintained. We smiled back—the boy contentedly. But I was uneasy. The same chill as had entered my body before I tore down the hill, now crawled within me, in the face of that smile.

We stayed with him, playing games, all afternoon. And they were the same games that we had often played, so happily played. The boy got into the same spirit of play as he had been in before. Now and then he would say, 'We don't play it that way father! Let me show you!' The father would allow himself to be taught. So the games went on, until we were thoroughly tired and the boy was thoroughly elated so that, when Kyanzo said that he would leave us for a few weeks, his little son cried, but I felt I knew. When he told me to tell Eileen that he was gone again, to tend his business, and would be back very soon, I *thought* I knew.

We watched him disappear over the mountain. The path was neither the one that led to the road, nor the short-cut that led to the market. Nor was it the one I had followed up and down the mountain. This was his own path, which he seemed to follow to his own unknown destination. We saw him last silhouetted against the sunset—a stooping mixture of determination and sorrow. And, looking at him, the boy said half in wonder, half in admiration and exultation, 'He played with me! Father laughed with me!'

I was lost in thought and only grunted, 'Um?'

'He has never played with me before!'

I nodded. But I could not answer when he asked, 'What happened to him? . . . Why is he not following the path?'

My mind, soul, every nerve of my body—indeed my whole being cried out in indignation against the one name—Gruff!

At the time when I was shaking with fury, the object of my indignation was propping himself against the white newly-painted pillar, supporting the wide verandah of his father's shop. He was flanked by a few students from Kyambe School who rented the rooms behind the shop, and a few market lay-abouts, all enjoying the warm sunset of a very clear day. Gruff was speaking, expounding a philosophy with words clearly not his own.

'As the saying goes, there are certain bows that can never be age-mate to the arrows that cross them. A lot has been preached about how every man is equal to everyone else. But I say that's not true.'

And, singling out one of the dirty and unkempt passers-by, Gruff used him as a target for expounding his theory.

'Surely,' pulling out a mousey-looking Kyambe School boy, 'you are not the same as *him* loitering on the road out there! Why? Because you are educated, you are clean, you know the standards of decency and hygiene . . .'

The selected boy stood there and fidgeted in the attitude of a cornered prey. Twice he tried to say something and twice Gruff shut him up with a flare of his philosophy.

'Can you tell me what the end of a man like that would be? Poverty! Misery! . . . people who will go to the grave without a mourner . . .'

More people came, attracted by his eloquence.

147

'But you . . . you are the lucky ones earmarked for the world of tomorrow, earmarked for leadership because you are decent and you are educated. We talk of progress, we talk of getting rid of the white man. But who can do that? None but us—the educated. Why? Because we know how! Yes, *we* know how! We know their language. We can therefore talk with them and convince them that this is not their land, that there are already enough educated men and women who can now lead, Christian enlightened men who can now own businesses and control our money. Take Kyanzo for example. Which white man in this country does not know and has not heard of him? None! Why? Because he has the biggest business any African could dream of. Show me the man who now can challenge him in leadership—None! But at that moment the passer-by who had entered the little shop next to that of the chief and had stood on the verandah and listened to Gruff, now stepped forward and said, 'There are!'

All eyes turned upon him, but soon reverted to Gruff. For the passer-by was ordinary. His clothes were ordinary. His hair, attire, shoes, in short, his whole poise, was ordinary—savouring of dirt, poverty and all the deficiencies that burden the lives of the poor struggling people on which politicians have capitalized, and upon which politicians have over-fattened since time immemorial. Encouraged by this mass rejection of the man and the consequent acceptance of his oratory, Gruff took courage and said, 'You see!'

But the man was not to be put down. Rapping his stick upon the hard cement floor, he blurted out: 'There are! I say there are, you . . . son of a robber . . A child . . . a stripling of yesterday, hardly weaned

148

from his mother's breast telling *us* this? And you all stand among these children, listening to these abuses! What kind of people have we become? Eh? I ask you what kind of people have we become?' He paused for breath and, almost choking with rage he blurted out: 'So none but the rich can lead? None but the chief— the owner of this shop here can lead people! Because he has money! Did you also tell these good people how your father amassed all this wealth? Eh? Did you tell them how he got rich by robbing and then impri- soning innocent women? Did you tell them how many people were silenced with death and oaths lest they revealed his wickedness?'

A murmur swept through the crowd. The story of their chief had been told and re-told behind closed doors. Now it was out in the open. Everyone of the grown-ups, who had lived through the time this old speaker referred to, now raised their voices and spurred him on, glad that they were not the ones saddled with the responsibility. More people came, and yet more. It was as if, by the sudden appearance of the old passer-by, all business came to a close. Everyone, buyers and sellers at Matuni Market was there, listening. Now the whole place was as crowded as it usually was when the white District Officer addressed the numerous barazas at moments of colonial crisis.

'Everyone here,' the old man began, 'even that small child there, remembers those days. We remem- ber those days when Bwana Mawe, the D.O. held the last baraza in this same market. And we all came from near and far, over the hills to hear him. We all remember what he said that day: that the white man had come to stay. It was ordained by God and no- thing could be done about it. Remember him saying

that the white man's might was shown in the way
he had routed Hitler. And you remember that no
mention was made of the thousands of our children
who were conscripted and transported to where the
battle raged fiercest—where they were placed in
the front line to take the first of the enemy's gunfire.
The war over, what happened to the white people
that had fought the war? Reward upon reward. And
what was that reward? Our land! All those grass-
lands where our cattle used to feed. And what did
our sons get? A pat on the back—a thank you from
the white man. Those that survived returned to
mend their broken homesteads without even a
gesture of help from the men we had gone to help. It
was this that made us heed the call of the fighters
who came to us by night—to drive out the white man
from the lands he had stolen. What followed, everyone here knows. Mass arrests, mass torture. But the
worst and the most vivid injuries that glared at our
faces was the mass arrest and torture of our women
. . .'

There were sounds of commiseration—and general
uproar. Everyone there remembered those days—the
haughty police armed with guns, bows and arrows
bursting into homes and arresting women, both the
young and old and whipping them up to Kyambe
police stronghold where they were locked up. Of
those that were released after the torture, only a few
ever talked about what went on behind those bars.
And even then, their reports were fragmented and
contradictory and no one knew what really happened
until the passer-by spelled it out.

'And in those cells they were tortured and made to
confess that they were all witches and had spearhead-
ed the oath taking. Many confessed. But even then

150

they were not allowed to rejoin their people. They had to pass before Bwana Mawe, the white D.O. and Chief Maundu, *his* father (indicating Gruff) for a final interview. And after that interview? A fine of three hundred shillings each. We all remember that fine—for which we had to sell all that we possessed to rescue our mothers and sisters. And where did that money go? Into the pockets of Bwana Mawe and Chief Maundu. That's how *your* father amassed all this wealth. And you, you stand there telling us that only the rich can lead . . . Is that what they teach you at that school of the white man?'

There was an uneasy and awesome silence during which Gruff fidgeted and sought in vain to extricate himself. For the crowd was all around him. At length, more out of fear than actual conviction he said, 'Listen old man, what you say is a lot of nonsense! . .

He did not finish. The wrath of the whole market was kindled against him and according to the school-boys who had stood and surveyed the scene from afar, the people would have torn him limb from limb had not Kyanzo's servant and Eileen, his master's wife, arrived upon the scene.

'People! People! Hold!' Hamad had cried, working his way towards the centre of the circle. Then he took Gruff in one hand and, paving a way out with the other, so that the three of them, Hamad, Eileen and Gruff, now stood facing the crowd, and said, 'What is this you do — killing a mere boy? He's big in body but a mere child.'

In the confused angry outburst that arose, the three would have come to harm, had the whole market-place not hitherto rung with the good deeds of this servant. When the crowd was silent the passer-by pointed at the chief's son and said, 'Young man, look at that man beside you and always thank him that he arrived in time. For, had he not, you would be surely dead.' He looked hard and long at the crowd and, turning to Gruff he said slowly and clearly, 'These dirty and torn people that you see before you are the makers of this wealth that you boast should lead us. We are the builders of that school where you are getting the education with which to scorn us. And it is our sweat that makes you sit, eat and sleep in comfort. We toil that you and your kind may be kept propped up and alive. For without us you are nothing but the clay from which you came. For you have never learned to earn a single cent by the sweat of your brow . . . You say that Kyanzo should be unchallenged in leadership because he has a business. What is that business? Selling vegetables? Does Kyanzo grow any vegetables? No! They are grown by that man there (indicating Hamad) and the likes of him—people like us. And all he does is come among us collecting them at a price depending on his whims. And we accept those prices because we must pay fees and taxes . . . and because the white man makes sure nobody but Kyanzo should sell vegetables. And you stand there with your handful of borrowed words and say *he* should lead us, because he has a business—Business! Ha!'

The passer-by spat as if to void himself of all like memories of business and went on his way.

Presently, the crowd dispersed, leaving the three standing alone in the market place. It was then that Gruff seemed to come to himself and surveyed his two companions. Sweat now stood upon his bruised forehead and uttering a horrified cry he turned and rode his motorcycle away from the market place, like a man possessed, leaving the two in perplexity.

The sun set as they left Matuni Market, and it was not until the full moon was high in the sky that Kieni and I heard them approach the house, talking and laughing as had now become their habit.

Kyanzo plodded on westward among the mountains, his heavy feet going *swish—crack— swish—crack* upon the grass and twigs. Now and then he would end up among the brambles, and only then would he snap into present time and exclaim, saving himself in the nick of time. Then he would relapse into the past wherein all his attention was imprisoned. He remembered that morning at Ngotheni when the tall athletic-looking man had stood before him in the main store. And after the door had been shut behind them, he could still hear the man's low, even voice as he poured out his story. Kyanzo looked keenly at that incident, recapturing all his feelings as they had been then: he liked that open face which appealed to his trust and as he listened to the story, the urge that had welled up in him to betray this man in rags and get the reward, died instantly. In fact, he hated himself then for harbouring such thoughts. The recounting of the murder of the little girl touched the rare chord of pity in Kyanzo's heart and he rose with the triumph of this man over Mnazi Mkavu. At that moment, Kyanzo had felt his power over Hamad, power to hide and keep him for as long as he willed and (what was then uppermost in his mind) power to protect this honest, simple man who had placed his life in his hands— protect him from those white men to whom he had to smile, be polite to and fawn upon, so that business might be blessed by their grace. In his innermost being, the protection of this servant against all the laws of the colonial power would satisfy the hollowness he felt for not being able to hold on to his

153

own, without having to pine and wheedle and play the chameleon. He, Kyanzo, would be the only law that Hamad would know.

So, Hamad had been sent to care for one of Kyanzo's petty holdings in the country—holdings which had been given to him by the Native Affairs office for being 'A most efficient and obedient native' or 'A polite native' or 'An intelligent native' or 'a Christian native' or anything of that matter which rambling old ladies and gentlemen saw manifested in this tall lanky native but which was as unexpected of him as the sweet water of Mara.

And here Hamad had performed so well that after six months, the master had at one time considered putting him on a minimum monthly salary. The land that had been all bush, brambles and snake hide-outs, had now turned into one dark earth on which the large lumps of soil rolled one upon the other. Where there had been a fruit garden of sorts, the fruits now glowed ripe from the trees as if to ask the master where all this care had been previously. In short, at the end of that six month period, the whole garden suggested a worker of unusual abilities.

Many a time Kyanzo would bring Eileen along, that she might witness the virtues of hard work. All this time, Eileen had been a quiet, meek and obedient woman, who never answered back. Between her and Hamad, Kyanzo had detected nothing but a cold distant dislike. Kyanzo therefore grew so confident in this master-servant relationship between Eileen and Hamad, that he at last decided that he could leave her at his Kyambe holding without too much risk, considering that both his son and the son of his friend were always there to discourage any untoward relationship. How then did this happen?

Again the picture of those two in the forest rose before him, mocking him: how she had held him tightly to herself, unmoving—how their lips touched and played and played. It was then that he became aware that that boy too was there. To kill them and hush it up successfully, the boy that was the son of his friend would also have to die. He would wait.

The sun had set over the hills far to the west, sending golden rays across the whole darkening sky. And behind those hills lay Ngotheni and a three year old newspaper called *The Coastal Chronicle* locked away beneath the money in his safe. A thin smile spread across his lips as he plunged down the hillside towards Matuni Market, where he would join the side road that led to the main road. And every step he took seemed to echo back to mock him: 'My wife! My servant! . . . A boy who knows it . . . My wife! My servant! . . . A boy who knows it!' . . . He plunged on through the quiet countryside, every nerve, every muscle of his lean lanky body taut with determination. He would not be responsible. No, not again!

When Hamad and Eileen finally arrived, they found us at different degrees of excitement. For my part I was bunched up like a cabbage for want of it. As she put down the green banana bunch that topped a large basket on her back, the little boy rushed to her, exclaiming.

'Mother! Mother! Father was here and we played with him—all day.'

Eileen did not heed him yet, until she had unpacked all they had bought at the darkening market, and until the boy had repeated his statement a second time.

'What *are* you talking about?'

To save myself, I took up the story and embell-
ished it with so many lies that by the time I had
finished, I was convinced there was not a greater liar
than myself. I said that Kyanzo had arrived about
ten in the morning, had been in a great hurry and
could not wait for them to come from the market
because business called him back, but that he would
be back within a few weeks . . . I lied, on and one,
putting as much distance between Kyanzo, myself
and that forest as I possibly could. But that wily little
imp would not let me get away with it. He recounted
the whole morning's activities with diabolical tho-
roughness, and by the end of it the adult couple
would have been fully convinced of my guilt, had I
not kept my presence of mind and said that—Yes,
Mutuo brooms were very hard to come by. I had to
look everywhere and the only place where I finally
met success was the bank of the river, way down
below us.

For a time everything went well and I thought
they were satisfied with my wanderings and efforts to
find a broom. But as the evening wore on, and the
whole significance of Kyanzo's mysterious presence,
his equally mysterious leave-taking and the alarming
direction he had taken began to dawn upon the
couple, we became quieter by degrees. Except for
Eileen's questions relating to the exact direction
Kyanzo took, the exact time he left, the exact words
he had told us, no other topic was discussed. Hamad
sat before the fire, pensive and subdued, as if all
strength had been drained out of him. At those times
when I would raise my eyes from the fire, I would
find his fully upon me, as if he read my mind as easily as he did his own irregular handwriting. Then guilt
would flood my whole body, from the roots of the

156

hair on my head, down to the soles of my feet. Thus we sat, each with his own thoughts, except little Kieni, who tried in vain to inject some happiness into the silent smoky hut, and was baffled that everyone remained so silent and distant. The fire burned bright and I wished it could burn away the cords of guilt that made it impossible for me to look upon the face of either Hamad or Eileen or even little Kyanzo, as I had done before. We all watched the pot bubbling upon it, as if that was our salvation. Hamad fetched his book and pretended to tackle an unsolvable arithmetic problem that took him all night to solve even though it was only 8 + 3 + 1. Eileen tried to sing, and the song dwindled into a hum and died away altogether. Then she applied herself to tending the fire which she harassed with unusual vigour. Thus we sat, until supper was ready. We clutched at our portions as if without it, we would be falling through endless space.

I excused myself and went to bed early. But I did not sleep, though what kept me awake I didn't know. Much, much later that night, I heard their footsteps come up toward the big house—and I heard Hamad say, 'He knows. I am *sure* he knows.' I strained to hear more, but Eileen's voice was low and muffled. Then I heard Hamad say 'Don't you see? This is the end!' And now Eileen's voice reached me, tearful and quivering, 'No don't say that! You mustn't say that!' They were still there when sleep overtook me—and I dreamed:

We were all on the athletics track at the school— all the boys in the school! I couldn't quite remember what it was we had to run for. But whatever it was, the thing was more important than life itself—we were all running and I was left behind, falling behind that compact group of legs that went up-down, up-down, in unison. Now I was very far behind and the track was no longer circular—its lanes now stretched and projected to the horizon, far, far away. Now the boys were at this horizon, drawing further and further away from me. Then I looked over my shoulder and saw—legs! Long, thin legs running by themselves a few metres behind me. I tried to increase speed, but seemed to be bound to earth. The legs were dangerously near, romping, romping. Then I heard Kyanzo's voice over the clouds, roaring as from a trumpet. I did not follow what he said but I *knew* the essence of it was that *I knew it and would pay for it.* The legs came nearer . . . nearer . . .!

I screamed and, terrified, jumped up into the sunlight of Friday morning.

Throughout that day, then the Saturday and Sunday that followed, both Hamad and Eileen kept to themselves so that Kieni and I felt more and more left out. On that Saturday when I went to wash my clothes to be ready for school on Monday, I took the path that cut across the new garden. Here, I found them sitting among the maize plants. They said nothing but were still, as if each must come to terms with the soil on which they sat. I have seen faces of many people, calm faces, agonized faces, happy faces, faces of all types, but I have never seen any face the like of those two on that Saturday morning—so still and yet expressing such a mixture of agony and happiness.

They were not aware of me as I stood hidden by the maize plants, looking at them—the two hoes with which they had been weeding, thrown carelessly across the path.

'Eileen,' Hamad was saying, 'This ought not to

have been . . . Because . . . Because . . . '

She put her soiled hand across his lips to silence him. At length, leaning against him she said, 'I have lived! Those few months I lived all the years I have not lived . . .'

'And it will end, Eileen, it will end,' Hamad said in a voice that hurt even my own feelings.

'Just when life has begun, it *must* end.'

'You must not say that! Look . . . I am here. I will always be here with you. You must not lose hope,' Eileen cried, her little fist clenched.

'Hope? There is no hope. All hope died when I placed my life in his hands. Now he knows about us, I feel . . .'

'But you can go away . . . another country.'

'No! That I cannot! I, we, belong here.'

'Then let's live every moment we can, before we face him. On that day let's not regret that we didn't live.'

I walked on to the river. In the afternoon, and long after the hour of lunch, I returned with my clothes washed and aired dry. Little Kyanzo was all alone when I arrived home and the pot he had been instructed to keep on the boil no longer bubbled, for the fire had long gone out. I took a wooden spoon and dipped it inside the pot. The maize and beans were hardly cooked and the water was lukewarm. I got furious and slapped him, calling him all the names and adjectives that indicate 'Sloth'. The boy let out such a yell, that I feared Hamad and Eileen would appear out of the blue and punish me, or that Kyanzo would suddenly appear as he had done two days before, and kill me this time. But none of this happened and I was safe until evening—when Kieni said, 'Mother . . . Kituku beat me.'

'He did what?'

'Beat me!'

'And what did you do that for?' she asked me. Silence!

'Eh? I'm talking to you! Have you ever borne a child, eh? Have you?'

I kept quiet, puzzling over the practicalities of the case.

'Or do you think because you go to that school there, you are licensed to beat people's children?'

Still, I said nothing.

'Eh? Answer! How dare you raise a finger against my child—you, whom I am supporting and feeding and doing everything for?'

And for the rest of that evening I was stood up in court and accused of waking up late; of being lazy; of being too talkative; of wasting too much paraffin when I did my homework; accused and sentenced; when that term was over, I was to pack up my things and go! I contributed nothing and was merely living upon their generosity. In short, I was suddenly the most unwanted being in that homestead or that vicinity.

At length she dished out the food and flung mine at me the way we flung the round disc in the school play-grounds, or the way we threw cast-off bones to a dog. I was so hurt by this gesture that I merely received the food, placed the plate on the floor and walked out. And for a long time I sat beside the house, listening to their easy chatter and jokes and laughter inside. Then I knew I was not wanted and my imagination showed so many problems connected with my staying there that I began to think of going back to my home to face the wrath of my father or decamping to Matuni Market and living by myself in one of the small rooms at the back of the shops. This idea had more appeal for me and I was planning how I would effect it, when Eileen burst through the door and shrilled, 'What do you mean coming to sit out here in the darkness? Are you eavesdropping *again* or are you bewitching us? Or is it our food you don't want.'

I had got tired of these accusations, so I replied hotly, 'If I eat, I am wasting your food. If I don't eat, I'm bewitching you. What do you expect me to do?'

She said nothing to this and, stamping her foot upon the ground as if she blamed it for my existence, went back into the house and shut the door behind her.

I rose and went to bed. And for a long time I lay there, wondering whether daybreak should find me in that neighbourhood, inexplicably hated as I was. I was shaken out of my thoughts by Hamad's entry- and I was struck by his silence. What was wrong with him? And what had happened to him? I wondered. At length he called out my name and said, 'Kituku— don't mind her! It's not her fault.'

'Then why did she tell me all that? If she doesn't want me here why doesn't she tell me to go without having to insult me?'

'I told you it's not her fault,' he repeated irritably. There was a period of silence and then he said, 'Little teacher, do they teach you about women up there at the Mission School?'

'No,' I said curtly.

'I wish they did. Then you would understand.'

'What's there to understand about her? Any fool can see that she hates me, that I've become a burden in this house and that she now doesn't want me—

though what wrong I have done I don't know.'

Hamad a-hemmed, and was quiet for a long time, after which he asked me whether I knew something called conscience. I replied yes. And did I know that it can kill a man? I replied that that was nonsense—a thought has no weapon, how *can* it kill a man? Then he said:

> *Afanyaye mabaya*
> *Hata yakamzidya,*
> *Na huku akahofiya*
> *Waja kumgundua,*
> *Huyo raha humwepuka*
> *Na moyo huteseka*
> *Mpaka mauti kumfika.*

To simplify it, he said that it meant it was the evil inside a man that killed him and not all the evils of others. I disagreed hotly with this, but Hamad merely laughed and said I should live a few more years—and this would be plainer. As to what had happened earlier that evening, I should forget it altogether for it was a passing whim with Eileen.

But the Sunday morning that followed proved Hamad wrong. After I had awoken and airily wished her a very good morning—(it *was* a very beautiful and clear morning) she merely looked at me and asked whether I heeded what she had told me the night before. To which I replied boldly that I had, and was determined to stay away.

That day I went to Matuni Market, in search of accommodation. As most of the shop-owners were at church I had to content myself with the shop-keepers' sympathies, 'Yes I am sure we can spare some space but then my boss isn't here, you see.'

162

It was not until after sunset that I arrived 'home', tired, hungry but successful, for I had found a room where I could stay. In return for this room and food, I was permanently employed behind the shop's counter, all Saturdays and Sundays. This was a much better proposition than living under a roof where I was not free from my guilty conscience, which intensified a thousandfold each time the inhabitants looked at me, and where my hostess hated every moment I trod the compound. Thus I arrived 'home' in the highest of spirits, whistling to assert my independence.

Hamad and little Kyanzo had just arrived from a walk in the woods, and the boy was about to go to the main house for the guitar, when I arrived. He stopped and, with the greatest hostility he could master, he said, 'Mother says you are leaving.'

'Yes,' I replied, 'Mother is right. I *am* leaving.'

'Are you going today?'

'Maybe.'

'And I shall then take your bed?'

'Maybe.'

'And all the sheets and blankets?'

'No! Those are mine!'

'But mother said I could have them and then I can sleep in the big house like a grown man.'

'Yes if you can grow up that fast and—of course—if you won't be afraid.' At this juncture Hamad hastily interrupted and said, 'You won't be afraid . . . little man . . . for I'll always be in the big house.' Then he seemed to have an afterthought for he quickly added, 'But then we . . . he . . . little teacher, will always be with us and . . . we three big men will always have the big house to ourselves . . . is that not so little man?'

But little man had definite ideas about who must

occupy the big house—which ideas he expressed by the weirdest pouting I ever did see, as he stamped up the little incline to the big house. Left alone, Hamad and I did not utter another word. This silence continued until little Kyanzo brought the old guitar and handed it to Hamad. The latter began to strum, but somehow he lacked vigour and, as I had heard those songs and enjoyed them before, I thought he did a very poor job indeed. His singing was now flat, as if he was trying to prove that he could still play. Presently he placed the guitar aside and sat silently in a very dark mood.

When Eileen learned that I was actually leaving, I heard her give a loud sigh of relief, which was followed by such cheerfulness, I wondered whether she was the same woman who had wanted me out of compound earlier that morning. For the rest of that evening, while we waited for supper to be ready, we played the old games and listened to the old songs by Hamad and it was altogether very pleasant. But I noticed that the looks and feelings that passed between them were still as incomprehensible and as intense as before. When we were ready to go to bed, Eileen accompanied Hamad and I thought that they took a very long time to reach the main house.

Nine

Third term in Kyambe Primary School! Third term in which the race for positions intensified, for it was always said that the third term in Standard Six, marked the dividing line between going to high school and to either a primary teacher's training college, or a junior agricultural college or (if the student had been lazy and stupid) an educated labourer's job at Mr. John Jackson's farm. Here this academic failure would shamefacedly sit in a dingy, dank enclosure, recording the bales of sisal as they passed before him. Often he would be found at the decorticating plant or among the sisal, cutting them alongside the other labourers who had never been to school. No place was as greatly dreaded as Mr. Jackson's farm. To us intellectuals, who looked down upon all manual labour and scoffed at it as part of the paganism from which we had been emancipated, Mr. Jackson's farm was the very abode of degradation and all that was low, mean, stupid and shameful. Often my father would use Mr. Jackson's farm to blackmail me into hard work. I would not be caught musing over the dust storms spiralling up into the heavens, without my father thundering about Jackson's farm in my ears. I would not take third position in any exams, without Jackson's farm rambling up from all horizons. Thus Jackson's farm became the dragon whose hot breath gave life to Kyambe Primary. At no other time was there as much of this dragon motivation as in the third term of Standard Six!

Notes were made, books were read and re-read, huge chapters in the Bible were memorized, arithmetic problems were tackled with renewed vigour and mental harassment; Rural Science became more and more incomprehensible in our attempts to learn the life history of Rural Skeletons—In short, no one would come into Standard Six classroom of Kyambe Primary without being impressed with the great intellectual horror upon the face of everyone.

I was now fully settled at Matuni Market and had firmly cemented my friendship with the various intellectuals who, like myself, were on a pilgrimage to Kyambe Primary. Together we had developed a firm pattern of travel. At four o'clock, when we had been released from school, the whole pilgrim contingent would run down the road to see who would arrive first. The same exercise was repeated early in the mornings of all school days. Owing to my diminutive size, I was always second from last. The last to get home was always a fat boy in the upper school whose lack of effort earmarked him for Jackson's farm—a dwelling he has not left since then.

Every Saturday and Sunday I stood behind the counter and sold from dawn to dusk. Many were the opportunities open to me for a little embezzlement. But I dared not, for too many voices of conscience played about my head. Thus I let pass by, many a good chance to enrich my pockets. I remember that eventful day when an old woman came into the shop with a hundred shilling note which her working son had brought her. She bought flour, vegetable oil and a tin of curry powder, all worth thirteen shillings and seventy-five cents. I had just given her the eighty shillings and was rummaging for the six twenty-five when, satisfied that sixteen five shilling notes were more change than she could bargain for, the old woman darted out of the shop and would have knocked herself against a passer-by, had I not called out, 'Mother . . . mother . . . your change!' The old woman looked at me in fright and would have run away altogether, had she not seen my bulging hand, extended towards her. Upon which she came back and asked:

'More? Mine?'

I said yes, and handed it to her. Then she told me to give her my hands and, holding them together, she spat upon them in gratitude and said, 'Let them as will stand between you and old age, perish thereof, confound them with the madness of the gods; let boils attend their anus and the fire of the gods eat their genitals. Let their path be a path of swords and thistles and let the rain of God sweep the very earth under them. Son, let my fathers keep you to the age of old Kilumo, who never dies and when you decide to, let them take you where no darkness shall touch you . . . pthu . . . pthu . . . pthu . . .!' She said, spitting into my hands which she held with her own fervent and trembling ones.

While all this had been going on, a few people had joined the buyers on the other side of the counter, including some of my classmates who made such faces at me that I felt ashamed. (One later told me I had become my grandmother's boyfriend!) These now fell to advising me about hygiene and, in urgent underhand promptings, they told me that I must wash my hands—for the old woman must have had a bad contagious disease, probably TB—else why was she so thin? And why did she cough? But an old customer buyer, having overheard this advice, told me in the sternest manner possible: 'If you are wise, young man, you will leave those hands unwashed. Do not pour cold water upon an old woman's blessing.' But this advice cost me the young customers who vowed that they would not touch anything handed to them by those dirty hands. And in the evening, when my two room mates and I sat down to read around the candle, they began to discuss that incident: 'Religion has made a big fool of you! Why did you give her back the six twenty-five? She would never have found out!'

'Fool yourself!' replied the other, 'What else could he have done?'

'Kept it himself! The old woman did not ask for it! She didn't even believe it was hers—He's a fool to have called her back.'

'But he got the blessing!'

'Blessing? Dirty hands, that's what he got! All the saliva and tobacco and toothless gums . . . ugh!'

But, whichever way we looked at it, this action brought me such good repute that the business prospered. In her gratitude, the old woman had used my good example to strengthen her village in good conduct. By the end of that term, so many stories had been invented upon the blessing that I did not run from school without the elderly generation taking that to mean high responsibility on my part and counselling their children accordingly. This reputation saved me from beatings which I was always expecting.

It happened that in the middle of the term, my father had come out to see how I was doing, whether I had recovered from Kyanzo's punishment and whether I yet trod upon the path or whether the pagan influence of Hamad had won over cane and morals. He had arrived on a Saturday in mid-morning to find no one at home except young Kyanzo who looked haggard and seemed to have got the idea fixed in his head that I was responsible for the neglect, the misery, the dirt, the hunger, and the general deterioration of his body and well-being. Upon my father's greetings, the boy looked at him and rolled those eyes as if to divine whether such a clean looking man could possibly be connected with so evil a rascal as I. Then he told out his story to my father: that mama

168

said I had left because it was all my fault, because I was lazy, I told lies, I played bad music that was not for Christians, I did not go to church, I beat him, I . . . did everything unpardonable from one who had been given succour, refuge and hospitality.

—Could my father see Kyanzo?

No, Kyanzo went back to Ngotheni and had not returned.

—Could my father then see Kieni's mother?

—No! she said they went to work and would not be back until very late.

—Would he know where they worked?

—No! They went that way!

But as the boy had pointed with all his five fingers spread out, and as two of those fingers indicated the heavens, and as no mortal man had ever gone up there except Enoch and the Prophet Elijah, he was at a loss as to where to locate the mistress and her servant. He opened his mouth to enquire of their whereabouts but found that the little fount of knowledge had vanished. Now my father was convinced that a small child could not lie—Kituku never lied when *he* was the size of *this* boy—for the child had not grown up to know the bad ways of the adult world wherein the Devil played chief instructor. Now I had done with the school of innocence and had been weaned into the Devil's own. What had happened to the good teaching of Kyambe School? What had happened to his son? He knew! It must have been the pagan influence of that servant; all pagans specialized in lies, in wrenching the youth from all ways righteous, and in re-directing them back to where they had come from through the original sin, even unto Sheol. Why hadn't his Kituku remained at home under parental guidance?

169

These thoughts crossed his mind as he hurried down the path, towards the market. He stormed the market, practically taking anyone he met under arrest and asking him one uniform question, 'Where does he live?', so that it was quite a long time before people knew what that pronoun denoted. As is characteristic of people when faced with strange phenomena, their curiosity rose to a pitch. As this strange man moved, so did they, until they reached the pavement outside the shop where I worked.

He found me weighing one kilo of sugar. Upon his bursting into the shop and my seeing the anger upon his face, I jumped up. He did not greet me. He did not greet anyone there. He did not even seem to see *me* at all. No! Behind that counter, he saw an errant bundle of evil in the wrong place doing something wrong for the wrong people and at the wrong time! Everything was *wrong*—and he sought to correct it!

'What do you think you are doing? Why did you leave the home I arranged for you?' I could not answer. Terror! Shame! The people murmured. Some laughed. Some commiserated. And some asked 'What! Is that *his* father?' My father was shouting, 'Come out . . . Here—Now—Kituku!—Come—here!' Sugar poured down . . . a woman screamed for her change— the weighing stones clattering on to the cement floor —murmurs . . . then I was in my father's hands.

But not for long! *The old woman was there!* She was talking to my father in words I dare not repeat and words he dared not listen to, all swear words. Obscenities ascribed to the whole of my ancestral tree . . . My grandmother and *her* son taking the greatest share. The people murmured that I could not possibly be wrong . . . 'Why? Can this *child* be so evil as to merit such adult anger? No! Can this child be so wrong to live in this place where he has shown such responsibility?'

'No.'

At this fiasco, my father had cooled down enough to listen to my employer's entreaties for a private conference. When they emerged, my father was much subdued and it was with an ordinary voice that he called me aside.

When we were alone, he told me to give an honest reason why I had left Kyanzo's hospitality. I told him of the sudden inexplicable change in my hostess's attitude towards me. I recounted my activities, of my studies, of my being Hamad's private tutor. At the end of the dialogue my father said he was satisfied and that he would see Kyanzo about it. He made me understand that Kyanzo had found him a good job at Ngotheni and he would be going back the following day.

'Back?'

'Yes. I have a job at the railway station. This is my second month now,' he said, and I thought I saw a smile trace across his usually tight-lipped mouth. I expressed my gladness and he took it in a spirit most unusual for him. Then he told me never to forget to attend church in which all good answers lay. Towards the afternoon he departed, leaving ten shillings in my pocket to supplement my earnings. I watched him disappear and I could not help being thankful to those people whom I felt inclined to call friends from the very rooftops—especially the toothless woman.

From that day on, my life assumed a definite routine in which the common denominator—hard work—was strictly observed. Often I saw Hamad.

Often I would invite him to my little abode, and he would survey it with sadness. Once or twice I ventured to ask after Eileen and little Kyanzo. His face would brighten, then cloud over and then assume a mask-like character—and he would not say much upon that subject. But I prevailed upon him to bring his guitar, in the evenings. On the Saturday before it happened, he played to us till very late in the night so that when he rose to go, I felt obliged to escort him home. And it was a very wild couple that traversed the countryside, singing the local songs that had been the cause of punishment a few months before. As we neared the house, Hamad became quieter and quieter so that when the iron-roof of the big house glittered in the moonlight before us, he was altogether glum. So I ventured to know the reason. But all he said was that I was too young to know, that, 'When you grow up and become a man, little teacher, you will remember this night, and you will remember that only a child can be innocent. And then you will forgive me . . . everything.'

I did not understand what he meant or what it was I should forgive him—perhaps because he did not stand up for me as a friend when Eileen changed her mind and expelled me from home. But I didn't contradict him, for he was talking again.

'You remember when we two came together?'

'Yes,' I said.

'And you, washing in the brook while I cooked . . . and the builders?'

'Yes!'

'And the music . . . all those songs?'

'How can I forget that!' I cried.

'Those were fine days, happy days . . . full . . . I almost felt . . .!' Here he stopped abruptly as if an

172

unseen hand had suddenly been placed over his mouth. Then he said slowly, 'It was a big lie, little teacher, to plan around what wasn't ours!' He mused for some time and, looking up at the star-studded sky, he cried softly:

'But soon now. I will come into what is truly mine . . . and that, no man may have but me.'

I didn't understand all these words but the sadness with which he said them moved me deeply and when the time came for us to part, he held my hands in both his and said that I had been a good friend to him, that wherever he went, he would always tell his friends, that I had been his teacher. Then he left and I looked at the bent, stooping figure of the man who was so strong yet who now seemed so weak, and wondered what had sapped all the will in him. I watched him move out of the cluster of trees and walk slowly towards the house. Then I turned, and with my mind full of the thoughts of all we had done together, I walked back to Matuni Market and was amazed when I found myself before the shops.

The days passed and, out of the fear of Jackson's farm, I applied myself to my studies with unusual industry.

The daily routine became more and more definite until Gruff broke it. The day was a Friday and I was running home to complete the home-work we were apportioned every Friday, when he overtook me on his motorcycle. And for about a half kilometre or so, it became a race between us. Now he would put his bike at full throttle and shoot out fifty metres ahead of me; then he'd reduce speed and zigzag along the road until I caught up and passed him. He would then shoot ahead, change his mind, race back towards me and around me. I did not realize what the relative

speed of the motorcycle was doing to my own and
soon I found myself running at top speed and out of
breath. Then I stopped, with sweat pouring down my
face. By this time Gruff had shot far behind. Now he
came racing at top speed and braked instantly beside
me. And he was grinning all over his face.

'Get up, little man, get up behind me.'

I refused. His scarred face perspired and he said
testily, 'I say get up!'

I refused.

'You won't eh? Good boy eh? Want to show a
good example to your peers—running home like a
maniac eh?' . . . he said, mimicking the old woman . .
'Well, I can also show a good example. Now get up
behind me . . . or else!'

I got up behind him and he drove slowly and in
silence.

'How is she?' he asked at length.

'Who?'

'Don't pretend, boy! How is she?'

'You mean Mrs. Kyanzo?'

'That's right!'

'I don't know . . . and I don't want to talk about
her. I don't see why you are so interested in her.
She's not your wife . . . And you didn't have to tell
Kyanzo the lies you told him—what would you gain
by it? What *did* you gain?' I cried indignantly.

For an answer, Gruff accelerated violently and I
would have fallen off, had I not held fast. Then he
braked suddenly so that my face hit his back and I
bit my lower lip. He stopped altogether and I jumped
off. And with his voice full of malice, he said between
his teeth, 'I gained a lot, little man, I gained much. I
gained the knowledge that a servant is dispensable.
All he can do is show off his strength . . . as your

174

friend did with my bike. But after that . . . what? Nothing? Even with strength he can be dispensable. He's . . . like a piece of soap, you can lather him to nothing! But you will emerge cleaner for it. You'll have something to show for it. A piece of soap has no voice! If you are stupid and careless, you can have lather sting your eyes. Even that wears off. Well, I am not so stupid, little man, especially with servants and I have seen very many of them Do you think Kyanzo likes what he knows? Do you think he likes it that I know and can tell everyone what I *saw*?'

Here Gruff smiled triumphantly. As he smiled my anger mounted. In my fury, he seemed to grow less and dwindle before my very eyes until he was level with me.

He laughed some more so that as I hammered him with my small fists, his laughter sounded like Kyanzo's on the day *he* left. Then he slapped me and I reeled upon the embankment on the roadside. Now he came towards me and I thought he had become a giant all of a sudden. I looked for a stone. None. My hands found nothing solid. In desperation I scooped up the soil with my hands, threw it in his eyes, and ran as fast as I possibly could. Just as I rounded the bend I heard the motorcycle start. Ahead of me were three men who were going to Matuni. I quickened my pace and overtook them. But I didn't pass them, so that when Gruff overtook us, he could not renew hostilities and I was safe for the moment. But the look this bully gave me told me that I would never be safe in the vicinity of Kyambe school, as long as he was there.

When darkness came and we had fastened the door of our little room, I found that I couldn't concentrate on my homework. My mind kept wandering between the fear of Gruff and the home where I had been a guest until a few weeks before. Now my mind was held fast by the image of Hamad walking home in the moonlight, the iron roof of the big house shining in that moonlight and the stillness of the night enfolding everything as if no one lived there and the two houses had become graveyards, and as if the tall eucalyptus trees stood guard upon that area, lest the spirits escaped from it. I made up my mind to visit this place on Monday evening. But the chance offered itself sooner than I expected.

That Saturday, I woke up earlier than usual. The birds were already up and singing. But nothing else was astir. I opened the door and slipped out. Up above, the stars were fading as the angry orange of the East brightened. Everything else was enveloped in a thin mist which covered the valleys and lowlands. The mountain tops jutted out from this general sea of white mist, like the heads of many bewildered ghosts. It was stinging cold and as I walked aimlessly along the pebbly road, my feet sent sharp, painful jabs of numbing cold up my legs. Still I walked, restlessly, going nowhere in particular. What made me walk, I couldn't define, save an unusual restlessness that forbade my remaining long in one spot. Gradually, the mist rose, wafting all around me and filling the air above. Then the sun burst out from beyond the eastern horizon, giving the mist a golden colour at its edges. And from somewhere inside that mist, the clang-lang-clang of the great Mission bell came rolling and rolling like the mist itself. The day had begun—and with it, my shopkeeper's work.

It was a busy Saturday morning and I ran up and down the whole length of the counter, now serving this customer, now that one. This stream of people continued until evening, about six o'clock. Looking out through the door, I could see the long shadows cast by the trees and buildings in the low sun out on the opposite hill, and I was musing about this when two unusual shadows crossed the floor outside the door. Heavy boot steps sounded on the pavement, rhythmic and (I thought) deliberate. Then the owners came into view. One was a white man, tall, lithe and in khaki uniform. To this day I still remember his eyes which were very small and bright blue. As he looked at me I felt as if the two eyes had become blades, twisting themselves through my insides to ferret out any ungodly thoughts that might be hidden there. The other was an African, like myself, in a red pullover, khaki shorts and heavy boots. On his head was a red cap. This man *always* kept just behind the white man's left shoulder and with the swaggering of the latter, I thought they must surely collide. Now the white man swaggered towards me and, using both left thumb and forefinger, he made signs that he wanted cigarettes. I brought out a packet. Then he indicated he wanted a light or matches. I produced the matches. He then indicated he wanted to know the price. And in perfect English I clearly pronounced, 'One shilling and thirty-five cents, Sir.'

The astonishment on the man's face was beyond belief. He looked at my head, and then at the counter, which was only a few centimetres below it as if he wondered whether I didn't mime the answer while the voice was produced elsewhere. But he quickly covered his surprise and assumed his steel composure. And, as professionally, he whipped out his purse and took out two shillings. When I gave him the change. he smiled and said no, that was for my good pronunciation of English, the best he'd ever heard in so young a native, and turning to his assistant, he asked whether that was not so. That's when they collided! As the assistant recovered from both shock and the question, he rapidly said, 'Yassah! Yassah!' in perfect parrotry. Now the white man turned towards me and put his hand on my head and playfully ruffled my hair. Then he asked for particulars of what I did, what school I went to, whether I didn't think going to school was better than remaining home in a *shuka* and looking after cattle all day in the cold rainy weather, whether I wanted to go to high school and which one—whether I liked the people there, whether I knew the neighbourhood. He asked all these questions in a voice that was not the same as when he had rasped at his assistant about my proficiency in English. It was now smooth and sugary and it reminded me of the tone of Reverend Wranglem often used at the moment when he played with his dog.

The white man went on. He said that many years ago he had worked near there and mentioned all the names of the people he had encountered, many of whom I knew. Our language was very nice to hear and was easy to understand. In fact a stranger should not find it difficult to understand—Didn't I agree? I opened my mouth and said in the best English I could muster, that indeed ours was an easy language to understand; that Reverend Wranglem spoke it fluently, that in fact he seemed to understand it better than—

I stopped myself short. But the white man was keen to notice my stop in mid-speech and I saw his eyes widen and shine with interest. He prodded me on, but I could not utter another word. Just then my employer entered from the door directly behind me upon which the white man bowed and in very awkward Swahili, he said that he wanted to talk to me, so that I might be his (the white man's) interpreter; which permission was granted with alacrity. We slowly went down the road, the three of us, now and then the white man stooping very low to hear what I had to say. I walked between them, and as we passed the last shop I saw my schoolmates grouped together, looking at me with envy and I felt very proud. More was my pride when Gruff appeared among them and stared at me with hostility and envy. Wanting to taunt them all, I cracked a joke—(a childish joke it was but it had the desired effect). The white man laughed aloud and ruffled my hair the wrong way, but in a most affectionate manner. More people had come out of their shops and out of the corner of my eyes, I saw them nudge one another and point in my direction for in those days a white man was a god and all his black associates were 'godlets'.

We walked on.

When we had rounded the bend and Matuni Market was lost to us, and had found that no-one walked upon the straight road before us, the white man stopped and grabbed me—suddenly. Then, from the inside of his breast pocket he whipped out an old newspaper cutting that was folded into a neat little square. Still holding me, he flapped the paper in the wind to unfold it.

'Look at this picture,' he snapped.

And in the dying light of that Saturday evening, Hamad's face stared at me. It could have been the face of a dead man but for the eyes that pierced and reproached me for what I was about to do. I started and fidgeted and tried to break loose. But the hand that held me seemed to carry some magic with it. A little more pressure and I went limp.

'Do you know this man?' he asked in a voice barely above a whisper.

'No,' I replied quickly. 'I've never met him, sir, never seen him, sir!'

'You know him,' he cracked and slapped me and I was sent reeling to the ground. For an instant I lay there stunned, and then thought of a plan. About ninety metres ahead there was a short cut that passed through the bushes. If I could reach it I would creep through the bush and warn Hamad in time. I got up and made a dash for it. But I had underestimated the assistant's zeal and power for I had not run fifty metres before I heard his heavy boots at my heels. A hand was placed on my collar, tearing all the buttons off my shirt. Then I was pulled back and slapped twice.

'Now look here you little bastard, you know where this man is hiding. Now talk!' the white man snapped.

I hesitated and he continued, 'Do you know what I do to little brats like you who refuse to carry my orders? I bind them and whip them. You wouldn't like that eh? Now talk! Where-is-he-hiding?' he said, slapping my face this way and that.

Pictures whirled fast before me . . . a girl beaten to death at a farm . . . a woman in the crocodile's mouth . . . caning on my bare buttocks . . . Kyambe School's house of Correction!

I talked.

The upshot was that I had to lead them and I led the way silently with every step I took echoing back at me, 'You fool, you little fool.' The white man stopped me and said I was to tell Hamad that Kyanzo wanted to see him urgently at Matuni Market. They were to wait for me in the cluster of eucalyptus that

180

bordered the compound. Should I fail, the white man would not only whip me. He would also hang me.

Slowly I walked towards the house. The smell of burning firewood reached me and I thought of the many many days that this smell had filled the air, the many days Hamad had made the fire . . . and I . . . walking towards his doom . . . every step I took prouncing doom.

The light of the fire streamed through the cracks in the wooden door, beyond which his voice rose and fell as he played his guitar as he had done so often before. I stood there, listening. It was the same song that he had played to the dancers and I, so long ago now. Still being sung in his own language. But now I thought his voice boomed out confidently, taking away some of the sadness with which he had sung the tune.

The song ended and Eileen's voice came, urging him not to play *that* song again. Then he said, 'I couldn't help it. Funny! I haven't thought of it for such a long time . . . I have forgotten some of the words,' and laughed. I knocked.

Inside the hut, it was suddenly quiet. Nobody invited me to come in. But the door was eventually flung open and little Kyanzo stood before me. I pushed past him and went into the room. The two let out a sigh of relief.

'Sit down Kituku and tell us why you haven't come to see us all these days,' Eileen said, genially, but her voice carried no conviction.

'Thank you but I can't stay,' I said, 'I have an urgent message for Hamad.'

'And where does this message come from?' Eileen asked, her whole body alert. She reminded me of a bush buck I had seen on the plains as the lion stalked her. I said quickly, 'Kyanzo!'

Both she and Hamad exclaimed simultaneously the one name 'Kyanzo!' At length Hamad asked, 'And what does Master want with me at this hour of the night?'

'I don't know. He just . . . told me to come for you.'

Then Eileen, seeming to come out of a long deep stupor, cried out.

'No! Don't go!'

'If Master wants me, I have to go!' Hamad replied. After a long silence he slowly rose and handed the guitar he had been playing to her.

'Master wants me!' she cried, 'What master? Haven't I set you free?'

'Yes but he . . .'

'What more freedom do you want?'

'You don't understand Eileen, but when he calls I must go. I must!'

'Hamad . . . what is it?' she pleaded, 'What is it that you never told me? You promised you would tell me everything. What is it you haven't told me.'

'He has power over me in my life . . . and I must go!' Hamad reiterated.

'Power . . . over your life? No man can have that. Whoever told you that?'

'Let's not argue over it, Eileen; I have to go to him; to confront him, to tell him about us . . . then I'll be free. Look; this can't go on all my life. I can't live with the shadow of fear hovering above me. I'll bring him here and we shall talk it out tonight when we come back. And then I will be free. I will make him understand. Then I can be with you always—without this torment of eyes looking at me . . . I must go and end it all—tonight!'

182

Eileen rose then and flung herself at him.

'Don't . . . Don't go!'

But he took her hand and gently put it down. She stood up and tried to bar the door. But he was already outside with me, close behind him. And when I looked back, Eileen was outlined against the doorway, with the guitar in her right hand—a fat beautiful woman in the early stages of pregnancy. Hamad now put his right hand on my shoulder and said, 'Let's go, my little teacher.'

And those words have remained with me all my life as much as the woman's wail that cut the still evening. 'How, oh, how shall we all live here now?'

He walked on, ahead of me, sure of his steps. Still sure of his steps, he did not seem surprised when the two figures stepped from behind the large eucalyptus trunks and ordered him to raise his hands, for he was under arrest. I expected him to use his great strength then and confound those two but, as if he had read my mind, he said quietly to the white man, 'I cannot raise my hands for fear of you or for a hundred such as you. A man can't run all his life. I have to explain and set myself free.'

Slowly and deliberately, he gave both his hands, not to the white man but to the African assistant. Whereupon, the latter looked at his master as if awaiting orders. The white man took the handcuffs from his pocket and handed them to the assistant. As they clicked home, Hamad's eyes were firmly fixed upon the black man's. Then the black assistant slapped him across the face once—twice—thrice, and barked something about Hamad's behaviour before his seniors.

When the sharp crack of the slaps had died down, Hamad replied in a clear voice, 'How can a self-made slave have any seniority? Such slaves don't even have the right to live and *you* talk to me of seniority?' And turning towards me he said, 'Little teacher, do me a kindness. Tell Eileen I'll never come back, . . . but I'll always be here—always . . . I'll always be here, for this has been my only home.'

He spoke the last word half tearfully, his face bright as he looked up through the space among the leaves, out towards the moon that shone above as she had always done upon the good and the evil, upon moisture and drought as if she said that to pin down one another upon the path of woe was the lot of men; that she had always seen this, ever since men made time, but that on the day men's hearts warmed and they learned to do well by one another, she too would wax warmer.

Later, when I told Eileen what had occurred, she gave one sharp cry of pain and looking at the door where he had trodden a few minutes before she cried to his vanishing presence, 'He's gone . . . Oh God of mercy . . . he's gone away from me!' and turning towards me she moaned, 'Why? Why did you do it?' over and over again. My protests that I hadn't meant to do it, that I had been forced to do it, were in vain and as I left her house, the words still rang in my ears, 'It had to be you! It had to be you—their interpreter . . . you, conceived and nurtured and taught by them . . . How much did they pay you? They gave my husband a business for being their slave . . . what will they give you—you that are so small . . . and stupid?'

Long after, and in the silence of the night, I still heard that voice with its bitterness and tears . . .

We reached Matuni Market. At first, the whole town seemed deserted and, in the soft brooding of the moonlight, the market assumed an eerie light.

184

We trudged on along the road which was the only street in the town. Presently we were joined by the market lay-abouts and the drunkards who had come to town from the villages so that it was a small procession that halted at the other end of town. Here the lights of an approaching vehicle glared at us and a Land Rover rolled in and parked off the right side of the road. We stopped here and the white man strode to the Land Rover. He spoke or rather barked at someone inside, for his voice was rough and had no warmth in it. Presently, four policemen emerged, followed by a tall figure which wormed out of the back seat and confronted the white man.

'So *you* came after all?' the white man asked.

'Yes. I had to see this, this . . . for the last time.'

The figure then strode towards us. And in that gait, I recognized Kyanzo. Behind him stood the white man, arms akimbo, and I thought he grinned, but of that I was not sure.

Now Kyanzo stood before Hamad, his face rigid. Only the lids of his protruding eyes seemed to move, as I looked at them, outlined against the moon. The two stared at one another, each unmoving. Then Kyanzo cleared his throat and with the venom of the cobra, spat the whole lump of sputum on Hamad's face. Slowly Hamad wiped his face with the irons on his hands.

'I could have saved you, you wretch!' Kyanzo hissed, 'Why then did you do this to me?'

Hamad said nothing.

'I thought I had always liked you as any master liked his trustworthy servant. You lacked nothing—food, clothing, shelter. I even gave you pocket money . . . kindness which many servants never had. Why then did you go beyond the bounds of this trust that

I had bestowed upon you; why did you come between me and my family?'

Still Hamad said nothing. At length, more out of fear of the silence than anything else, Kyanzo said, 'What I have done I have done for the evil you have repaid me. God cannot hold me accountable for what will happen to you. Your own evils: murder, lies, adultery—those will be your judges—not me.'

Then Hamad spoke.

'You say that God cannot hold you accountable for selling me—yes, selling me to him (pointing at the white man). What right do you have to hold judgement over my life? What I did, I did because there was no other way, because no one could speak up for me, or those enslaved labourers on that farm and no one stood up for the defenceless girl who died trying to save her own mother. For that deed I have no remorse. Let that god you call upon to witness search my heart. In the face of the brutality I witnessed on that farm, no law can condemn me before condemning all those who hold their fellow human beings to bondage and death—people like this white master here who have failed in their own homes and now come to us to prove they still are men—people like you who have let life be drained out of them by conniving and drivelling and bending lower than the lowest beggar of Ngotheni town—for a few pieces of fake silver in their pocket. How much are they going to give you? A fat wad of money? A business? A pat on the back—slave's wages! And all for what? To still the echoes out of your emptiness—Because you and every fool like you who live by black-mailing people into submission, are empty. And you are the emptiest of them all—you are even empty of life itself and have lived a life of suppression—even that of your family

186

itself. How then can you talk of love? How can you stand in judgement over me? I killed that white man! Perhaps I didn't plan to do it then. But now, looking at you and all fools like you who live borrowed lives, I am glad I did it. And as for what you charge me with, if there was not evil in the hearts of each man and woman alive, that could not have occurred—the evil that makes us look at other men and place labels upon them—the evil that makes us tell we are better than other men, the evil that we cannot respect one another, love one another, help one another—the evil that we treat one another worse than animals. I can't apologise to you for what has passed between me and her. For you would surely trample upon that sincerity as would a pig upon gold.'

Kyanzo hit him then. As he hit him a cry went up from the people gathered round. Here and there I heard both Kyanzo's and Hamad's names whispered.

Hamad did not cry out—and Kyanzo hit him again —drawing a loud angry protest from the people. Out of the small crowd, a man stepped forth and tottered drunkenly to where the two stood.

'Lissen—Kyanzo.

'This . . . this man's my friend . . . talked to me when I us't build your house. Didn't finish it, you bastard . . . If it's true he did it to your wife . . . I am glad . . . Needed it . . . you are empty of everything except money. What you braggin' about—an empty thing hitting a man like this!'

The crowd went wild with laughter, which made the black assistant snarl at them.

'Take him in!' the white boss hissed. The last I remember of Hamad was him standing against the Land Rover. He stands there still, and calls me to him. And I still hear his voice as I record these things.

'Little teacher, do not blame yourself. Even without you, Kyanzo and this white man would still have found me. For they can't bear to think that any man of another breed can bring them down. They *must* win. And that's why I must go. But wherever I am, I will remember you. I shall remember my little teacher. You taught me their magic words with which they have enslaved us. Teach. Continue to teach always. And always strive and learn to teach the way to bridge the gulf between men. For on the day when there is understanding between all men we will be surely free. Then no man shall die at the hand of the slave master. Then no child shall cry and die of hunger . . .'

'Get going you!' the black assistant roared and, helped by the four African policemen, he pushed his victim up and into the Land Rover. That was the last I saw of him.

The white man sat in front against the window and as the Land Rover started, he said, 'Mr. Kyanzo, come to the headquarters tomorrow and we'll square it.' Then the Land Rover picked up speed and I gazed at it as it disappeared into the moonlight—taking him away—for ever.

For a moment, it was silent, as if all speech, all sound had suddenly gone with him. Then the crowd began murmuring among themselves and gesticulating wildly. The drunk now called for Kyanzo to show forth. But he had disappeared. Some said he had slunk up the hill, while others said he had hurried down the road towards his home. No one was sure.

When all the people had dispersed, I was left standing where the Land Rover had been. I estimated that my head was level with the door of the vehicle and I tried to have him speak to me again. But all I could hear then was, 'Then no child shall die of hunger' over and over. I saw him then. At first it was his back as he cycled uphill and downhill; then him playing the guitar, laughing, working together . . . a young boy standing on a bridge . . . a crocodile . . . blood upon the waters . . . Eileen pregnant, standing in the doorway.

I tried to go to bed, but couldn't. I felt as if I must wander about and find him, to have him speak to me again, to impart some of his simple conviction to me. So I walked the road like one possessed, without knowing what I did or whither I went. All I was aware of was the bright moon up above and the general awesome dark shadows of the landscape. It was deathly quiet. No cicada sang upon the tree, nor the cricket, nor the bird of the night. The air itself was silent. I sat down on the side of the road and tried to call him. For, at school, someone had said that if we sat silent and called insistently, hard and loud enough within ourselves, that for which we had called, would surely come. I tried to conjure up the prison into which he must go. I saw him seated in there, in the dark. I made a great effort and flashed the light into the prison. Then I made the judge send for him and heard him say, 'Muhammad you are free. Your mother and your sister's deaths are enough to buy you free. Behold the door opens and you shall walk forth, free of the domination of any man over you . . . Go your way and God be with you.' I made the doors open and Hamad come running . . . running home. I made Eileen meet him on market day and saw the smiles upon their faces. I made them work upon the field while I held their little child in my hands. I saw the storm again and made the river overflow and I took Hamad to the bank to look at it, for

I must cross it to reach my school. I made Hamad say, 'Use the swing the way I taught you!' And then I saw myself on the other side shouting victory to him . . . 'I have crossed the river! Hamad! I have crossed the swollen river.'

Suddenly, I came out of the dream. From the direction of the hills, a long re-echoed scream reached me. Then it was repeated again. Now I heard another one join in and both screams became louder. I ran down the road and took the path that led to Kyanzo's home. What I found there is best described by Kieni's autobiographical sketches, which he has kindly allowed me to include in my story.

'When Kituku had betrayed him and they had led him away, my mother became like one possessed. She came into the middle of the room where she stood, his guitar by her side, like a new child that was learning to walk. I asked her whether I should shut the door for the chill was creeping from the mountain above. But she did not answer. For she was not aware of me. All she said was "For the first time, since I knew I was a woman, I felt alive. My life had began to have a direction and a purpose—someone to care for, to help, to love. Now . . . it's gone! You are gone . . . gone."

'She burst out of the house and into the bright moonlight, and wandered across the field where we had so often played our games. She would re-cross it as if he was there and still playing hide and seek. I called her but she could not hear me.

'Often she called upon him to come and touch her, to hold her, to give her strength. Then like one sleep-walking, she rushed down in the direction of the new garden where they had so often worked together among the maize, green then but now nearly ready

190

for harvest. I followed her from a distance, afraid that she might harm herself. The crackle of drying maize leaves led me to where she had stopped, looking intently at a spot upon the ground. Here she stood still and addressed that spot, as if a human being was there. Then she stretched her hand upon it and said, "Thank you . . . " and then "Now I am alive, and can never die. For the life you have brought, I will thank you for all time. Tell me about yourself . . . everything. Don't hide anything."

'There was a pause and then she began to sob and weep like a little child and I looked at the convulsions of her body and the way she tore at her hair, and I wept because I felt that my mother was mad.

'The moon was high in that clear starry sky and she addressed it as if it knew what was happening here on earth.

' "Good-bye, Good-bye. You that brought life to my sleeping soul—good-bye . . ." She cried this . . . on and on clutching at her breast. Then she would bend down as if he lay at her feet and pass her hand gently up and down the space below her. At times she would laugh aloud and answer, then ask questions as if the earth at her feet had sprouted lips with which to converse. Then she rose and burst out weeping and retraced her steps home. I followed her back into the house where we sat, saying nothing. At length, out of unease more than anything else, I picked up the guitar and began to rumble it in the darkness for the fire had long gone out. She exclaimed, poked the fire and re-kindled it, and in the blaze she saw that it was only me. I saw her tear-stained face then and I panicked. Those eyes were not the eyes of the mother I used to know. In the glow of the fire they seemed brighter than usual, darker than usual. And all the while she trembled as she had done so many times at Ngotheni town, when the fever was upon her.

' "It's only you!" she exclaimed and before I could answer, she barked at me, "Get out, Kyanzo, Get out!"

'I dropped the guitar and slunk out, for I thought she was out of her mind. I slunk out—into the presence of my father!'

'He towered above me, his face a silhouette against the bright moon up above and I feared. Then he brushed me aside and stood in the doorway, facing my mother. She did not heed him, but sat trembling still, and staring beyond the walls of the house. My father slowly bent down and picked up the guitar and for a long time he looked at it, up and down, up and down with a demonic expression, (halfway between laughter and murder) upon his face. He rumbled it as I had done, and my mother turned her eyes. For the first time she became fully aware of him. Then, as deliberately and as menacingly as he had walked into the house, my father picked up a string and ripped it off with a loud twanging sound. My mother pounced upon him then and fought to get it from his hands. But he shoved her aside and continued to wrench the strings off. When all six dangled from the tuning buttons, my father threw the whole mess down at her feet where it clattered with the sound of any empty tin. Trembling, my mother stood up and confronted him, "You . . . animal! You animal!"

' "Oh, the relics of your pagan lover eh? Eileen, we have been married for a long time now. I have shown you the way of righteous living. Before I went away I told you to be responsible; to understand and rule this house. But above all I told you clearly never to step aside from the righteous path along which we followed, you and I, and which has been the basis of *my* success. I told you never to forget your duty to the church which would protect you from the evils of the pagan life we have left behind. But you chose to go against my wishes and now look what you have done to my home, you . . . whore! Now Eileen" . . . My mother looked at his face and spat at him.

' "Eileen . . . Eileen . . . your church, your baptism your righteousness . . . I am not Eileen any more. My name is Mumbua; that's the name my mother gave me. And I lived happily with it until you married and killed me to prove to the white men you could be like them . . . for money. Yes, you killed me! What is a married woman without children. All I have is one child . . . begotten of luck. For years you have imprisoned me. You have denied me the right to go out and meet people, for you were always afraid . . . afraid that others might look into my soul and see its drought, see the prison into which you have shut me. You have denied me the right to work, to be responsible for anything that might bring back the self-respect I lost the day you put this ring upon my finger to stifle and strangle me. You have packed me into church where I have been blackmailed into obeying you as a wife ought a husband. And for a long time I have sat there and listened to words that could not have the slightest meaning to me. In the old days, if a man was not a man his brothers built his home. But even there you had nothing. You were born alone, a man without a relative. You have always been without your people . . . and I didn't know what you had done to me, the happy maiden that walked into your arms after you gave me this . . . ring (here she threw it into the night)—until I found him. . . And he set me free! For he has a heart that beats and feels. Now you have sold him . . . Take your death-ridden life away from me . . . die alone like the lonely empty creature you have always been." She stared at him, panting, then.

' "Do I look weak and withered, controlled, beside the grave? I refused your prison. I defied your death . . . I am back from your grave and look . . . I will soon be a mother. How can you come back here and claim me, you that died so long ago? What do you want of me when you are less than a man? All you can do is kill, betray, hold others down by black-mailing them. Did you really think you could ever be as much a man as he was, you whom money and strange people and their religion have burnt out? What do you know other than wheedling, selling people for a reward? He was a man! He had a human heart and I loved him . . . I loved him," My mother cried then, the tears running down her cheeks.

'My father stood still, like one petrified. Slowly, his stiff angry hands reached up to her neck, and as they closed around it, my mother looked at him and said through her tears, "You can kill me. But that won't make you any more of a man, nor wipe out what you have done to me."

'I saw his arms tremble and I screamed as much as my lungs would allow. Then he seemed to become aware of me, for he let go of her and turned. My mother screamed so that my father was in the cross-roads of our screams. Slowly his hands went limp at his sides as he walked out away from the house.

'When he had gone, we closed the door, bolted and secured it and we sat huddled together in fear, my mother's arm around me. How long we sat there, I don't remember. All I remember is hearing light foot-steps outside, a knock on the door and Kituku's urgent voice that something terrible had happened . .'

*   *   *

I had followed the path up the hill, my heart
pounding heavily. The screams were very distinct
now. Soon after, I saw a figure approaching me from
the direction of Kyanzo's house. I hid in a cluster of
shrubs and waited. Presently the figure passed—and
I recognized Kyanzo again. Behind him, the screams
still rent the air. But I was more interested in this
man and what new plans he was now hatching. I
followed him, thinking that he was going back to
Matuni. But he didn't. He branched off and took the
path that led to Kyambe School. I wondered what he
wanted there and at this hour of night. I was soon
disabused, for the man didn't seem to be going anywhere in particular. Now he'd stop suddenly and stare
all around him as if he expected to meet someone he
dreaded. Then as suddenly, he would resume his
wandering. In this manner, we came to the river,
whose murmur was audible from afar in the silence of
the night. Here Kyanzo stopped and sat on a large
rock that jutted out from our side of the river bank.
He sat there, looking at the plunge pool far below
him, his chin and left brow planted in his large left
hand.

For a long time he sat there, barely moving his
head, staring fixedly at the water far below. Then he
seemed to want to get up and he tottered unsteadily
like one heavily drunk.

'Look out!' I shouted involuntarily. But it was too
late! He reeled and, with a long drawn-out cry of
terror, he fell over and splashed into the pool. I ran
to the rock where he had been sitting and looked into

the water. From the spot into which he had fallen the water still frothed and rippled out to the far edges of the large pool. The reflected moon seemed to dance, play hide and seek and laugh in these ripples. Then the pool was calm again and the round face of the moon was fully reflected with the woman who was supposed to live there, featuring prominently in the pool. Still Kyanzo did not come up. I called and called, but still he didn't come. My voice came back to me in a thousand echoes. Far below me, the deep pool lay quietly like the mouth of a large monster that waited to devour me. I was reminded of Hamad's mother and the beast of the waters and, in deep mortal terror known only to children, I ran up the path as fast as I could, and did not stop until I reached Kyanzo's house.

It was Sunday. Long before Eileen or Kieni had woken up, I was on the path that led to Matuni Market. There were very few people on the road. But whoever I met, I told the news of the tragedy. Finding very few people in Matuni, I decided to run into the village and tell the old men. They would know what to do.

We gathered on each side of the pool in mid-morning. The diver who was going into the water for the second time, braced himself for a dive. He remained under water for a long time and we were becoming convinced of his fate when he burst out from the middle of the pool.

'Found him?' an old man asked.

'No. This pool is like one gigantic pot with stone walls on either side. I followed the wall until my feet and hands froze—and still I could not reach the bottom,' said the diver.

'Go to the other side,' the old man pursued. 'It is

taboo to bury a man under water.'

The crowd murmured assent and, rallied by this, the diver took a large gasp of air and went under water. Again the long silence. At last he came up.

'Found?'

'Yes . . . I think have. But he is too far down there. All I felt were his feet. The head and the rest of the body are caught up among roots.'

'Then rest a while and get him.'

'I'll need some help. If I disturb the pattern of those roots without any help, he might be freed and then he'll be gone completely.'

'In that case he'll float.'

'Not likely,' returned the diver. 'That pool seems to expand into an underground drain. I tried to swim to where the head was but I found myself being pulled along. I will need help.'

It was early afternoon when the second diver arrived. About two hours later, both men emerged with the body between them. The crowd let out cries of sorrow and gasps of astonishment—for the remains of Kyanzo made a ghastly sight. His body was swollen and the eyes that had bulged and stared before, were now sunk deep into the swollen face.

I went nearer and looked down at the body and despite my former feelings towards him, pity and sorrow flooded my heart for him. Dead, the body seemed to radiate messages of helplessness and dire need of pity and care. And I shed tears for the stranger who had stood before me, many months before, and who had accepted me as one of his household. My mind reeled over the times he had been with us and then I was convinced that whatever he had done to me, the harsh words, the beating . . . were all part of the same intention—to do well by my father

(who was his friend) and by his friend's child that was
me. I looked at this body and I knew that good
intention can become warped in application so that
the end result is evil. I forgave him then and, deep
within myself, I wished him a safe journey wherever
he should go, now that his body was no longer his
burden.

Eileen was there too and if anyone looked at her
face, he would not have discerned anything concerning her feelings. She stared down at the body like one
in a trance and one to whom the life now and
beyond, had intertwined in one confused tangle, and
I wondered whether she was aware of the part she
had played in bringing this about. Only Kieni cried
throughout and called out, 'Father!' in between sobs.
And looking at that child then, and knowing the
harsh treatment he had received at the hands of he
that was dead, I was convinced it was true that none
had a heart so free, loving, forgiving and without
malice as the child.

A message was dispatched to my father at Ngotheni informing him what had happened and request-
ing his presence at the burial, the following day at
four o'clock.

Members of the church and any close friends of
Kyanzo were asked to remain behind to comfort the
widow and orphan and I was astonished that only
three people, the pastor, the choir leader, and one
woman (a member of the church choir) remained.
And I puzzled over this scarcity of friends until late
at night, when I fell asleep.

That night, I dreamed about them. Hamad seemed
to rise from behind the mountain overlooking the
place where he had worked. His hands were in chains
and when he had come up to the mountain top he

stretched his right leg across the abyss and placed it on the peak of the opposite mountain. And standing astride, he grew larger, heaved and swelled, and with one gigantic muscular effort he wrenched the chains asunder. Now large drops of blood trickled down the chains on each arm and as they touched the ground of the valley far below, spurts of smoke arose. And then I looked closely and the smoke came out of the ground where Kyanzo puffed at his pipe. It was dark then so that Hamad's body was hidden by it as if it was thick mist. Only his face remained, his eyes looking at me and he kept jingling the chains and, smiling, he said, 'Little teacher . . . go on . . . go on . . . the way is open.'

During parade on Monday the headmaster announced that in the afternoon the whole school would assemble and go to the home of grief to help lay the body to rest. All that morning I could not concentrate on anything and I was glad when the lunch-break arrived when I went to sit by myself at the base of an eucalyptus tree. At the sound of footsteps behind me I turned and came face to face with Gruff.

'What are you doing here? Hiding in your guilt?' he tormented.

'Leave me alone!'

'Leave *you* alone! The good little boy, the good example of Matuni Market—turned Judas Iscariot, leading the police to the arrest! What price your boasts now? Wait till they all hear what you did, and how it was all your fault that that servant was arrested,' he said this breathlessly and I detected a note of fear, horror and lack of conviction in his voice.

'You leave me alone! You can go and tell them. But that won't wash away your guilt in this affair.

Who pretended he was Kyanzo's friend and told him about his wife and Hamad? You! Who made Kyanzo sell Hamad to the white people? You! And you tell me I am Judas! Who is Judas now? Who led Kyanzo to his death? You can accuse me before all the people but since I know who is behind it all, take care—my friend.'

Gruff stood still, like the trunk of the tree on which I leaned. I saw fear in his eyes and he that was almost as tall as Kyanzo and was the terror of even the highest authority in this school, dissolved into a trembling child. Gradually, he composed himself and said, 'You tell them, and then you'll know who I really am.'

He went his way and I didn't see him until the burial that evening. Then I noticed that he kept looking at the coffin and then at me with haunted, horrified eyes. And I was certain that I was the instrument of that horror, that I was not safe as long as I was in his vicinity, and that this dead body would haunt him as Hamad's shadow had haunted me at night.

My father was there and when the time came to pay tribute to the dead, and he had been called upon to make his speech as the dead man's friend, I saw him shed tears. He could not go beyond the words, 'He was my friend and an upright man. He always stood by me like a true friend. When I needed his help, it was readily available. He gave my boy a home . . .'

Everyone looked at me. What did they think? Why did they look at me like that?

Towards sunset, the body was lowered in the grave and after Reverend Wranglem had preached about how we came into the world in tears, lived in tears and went back home in tears and how we believed we were always with a comforter, he threw a handful of dust on the coffin. Then he said that our bodies came from the dust and to dust they must return and that all those of us who lived should take example from this and know how weak and transient we were, that we might do well by one another now. Amid the song 'God be with you till we meet again', interpersed with wails, the grave was covered and a white cross placed upon it. I looked at each one assembled there and upon each face was written the mark of sorrow. As we left, I puzzled over what the Reverend had said, and why it was that we always waited till it was too late before we had compassion and love for one another, why we hated, betrayed, killed and subjected one another to misery if the end result of all the evils of this body was this grave? Why didn't we see even a year ahead of us?

AFTER ...

It was harvest time and we would soon be on parade at Kyambe School. It was early morning and I sat in the headmaster's office as I had done so many weeks before. The white woman who dominated everything by her position high up the wall, still looked at me quizzically as if she demanded to know how much I had learned that year. Her hair still burned on one side like the burning bush of Sinai that was never consumed to ashes.

Headmaster Mathayo came in and, pacing deliberately behind his desk, he sat down and looked at me. But now there was no hostility in his eyes, nor any trace of authority in his demeanour. Ever since the death, he had become more serious, thoughtful and kinder. And in his walk there was not any more

201

the rampant, angry stride of authority that increased the terror of the cane. He was just a man, doing his job as he read the letter in his hand.

'Well Kituku, your father wants you transferred.'

'Yes, sir.'

'Do you want this transfer?'

'Yes, sir.'

'Why?'

I kept silent. How could I tell him that I was afraid of Gruff? That I had to leave this scene of memories?

'Is there anything in this school that makes you want to transfer?'

'No, sir,' I lied.

You had to be a great being to tell *your* headmaster that despite his concern for other's misfortunes, yet his rules, his strictness, his potential reversion to nastiness, all made and compounded these fears and hatred of Kyambe School.

'Speak the truth. What was it you did not like in this school?'

'Nothing, sir,' I cried hysterically.

'How well did you do in your exams?'

'Well . . .' I hesitated.

He pulled out my file and thumbed through my examination papers.

'English 83, Bible 81, Rural Science 70, Geography 92, Arithmetic—13! Good grief! Thirteen!'

And exclaiming he went through my arithmetic paper, question by question. At length he said, 'Everything is right until the answer . . .

'How *could you* have got all the answers wrong?'

'Well . . . sir, I felt I was . . . solving the wrong problem,' I mumbled.

'The wrong problem! What on earth do you mean?'

But I could not explain. All I said was that I could

arrive at no answers. Upon which the headmaster noted that I had been acting strangely since the burial and asked whether that had had anything to do with my arithmetic paper. I said it may have had but that I didn't know.

When totalled, my marks placed me fourth in the class, as the headmaster informed me. But if I had arrived at the right answers in my arithmetic paper, I would have been top of the class by twenty-six marks. Did I want the arithmetic teacher to reconsider?—No. I wasn't interested in coming top of the class?—No . . . All I wanted was to be allowed to go and help the harvesting and then to go away to my home. And this turned out to be the only good thing I did in Kyambe School. For, after the headmaster had asked me where I wanted to go harvesting, and after I had informed him that Kyanzo's widow needed help, for she was now all alone, Mr. Mathayo sat silent, looking at me intently. At length, he said that I had surely learnt the Christian principles upon which Kyambe School was founded.

During morning parade, the headmaster said that the school had a great reputation for its uprightness and adherence to maintaining the principles of charity and good neighbourliness; that it was now the season of harvest and that we ought to take compassion on the woman bereaved a few days before. He therefore ruled that because the staff were all busy adding marks and arranging class positions, we should all go across and help the woman and her son in harvesting. So for the rest of that day we ravaged the maize garden where Eileen, Hamad and I had cleared those many days before. I have never seen anything as pleasant as all those hands, all six hundred of them, working among the dry, crackling maize plants. Never did I hear anything as sweet as the sound of the laughter of all those boys as we harvested. But above all, I have never been more satisfied with myself as on that day, when I saw Eileen smile again as she saw the activity on the garden and the long, long column of boys who passed the maize cobs from hand to hand right up into the big unfinished house that now acted as the granary.

Towards evening the garden had been cleared of all the maize plants, which were now neatly stacked. The wind played upon the field then, ruffling and sweeping the empty husks in the same attitude of play as the four of us had played in the season on the rains.

When we had finished harvesting and were ready to go home, I found that the headmaster had, unnoticed by us joined in our youthful energy. He was now talking to Eileen about the state of the 'granary', that the house needed completion and that if she had the material, the school would help out in completing it. We all pledged in one chorus that when the time came, we would surely be there to help. I never stayed long enough in Kyambe to participate in the completion of the house but on that evening I stood on the same ground where I had stood before and looked at the school. For a moment the picture of the solid wall of rain falling upon it flashed through my mind but it was soon gone. I looked at those iron roofs of the school, bright in the low sun and then I was momentarily sad that I was leaving it.

When we were all ready to leave, young Kieni emerged from the house, accompanied by one of the boys who had been punished for going to the 'primitive' dance. And in Kieni's hand was the wretched guitar now very ugly, the strings dangling. The schoolboy sat on the verandah and, supervised keenly by

204

Kieni and unaware of the headmaster's interested scrutiny, the schoolboy re-stringed the guitar and tuned it. Little did I know that this little action would shape the whole life of the man-child that Eileen then carried within her.

We were the last to leave the house: the headmaster, the boy who tuned the guitar and myself. When we came to the river, we found about fifteen boys swimming in the pool, laughing as they played hide and seek. The headmaster lost his temper then and would have caned them there and then had they not swum quickly out of the pool and dressed in such haphazard panic that even he had to laugh. For some of them put on their clothes inside out while others struggled to put on their shirts with their heads trying to pass through the shirt-sleeves. The headmaster never punished them. But he issued a stern warning that the pool was from now on out of bounds to any boy of that school. On the following day, Tuesday, we all went to the pool and built a formidable fence of thorns around it. To my knowledge, no one has ever swum in that pool since my colleagues did the day before.

I left Kyambe school at the end of the term, determined never to return, and joined Ngotheni Primary School near where my father worked.

The years rolled by and with their passage, my curiosity and desire insisted that I should revisit the place that had made so deep an impression on me. But it was not until last year that I finally did drive down there.

The two houses still stood but both had been fully roofed with iron sheets. Out of the big house, an elderly woman emerged. She still had the same bright eyes and the same smile. She did not know me, and eyed me with such curiosity that I could see that she was trying to trace my face to some time in her history. I was about to introduce myself when a tall youth emerged out of the smaller house, saying, 'Mother, hurry up. I'll miss my bus.'

At the sight of him, I gasped and started involuntarily. For Hamad stood there, every inch of him except that now he was younger and browner. Then Eileen recognized me and smiled. It was a smile that said so much and I could merely nod.

That afternoon Rudia (for this was the youth's name) came with me to town, his briefcase on the back seat of my car and a twelve string guitar under his armpit, his fingers always on the strings. Throughout that journey, we didn't say much for he seemed to be preoccupied with the sad song he was playing. So I didn't know his destination or what he would do when he got there. But the total of the little he said could be summarized by his song and his short sad utterance! 'Looking for home.' And as I drove to my own house I thought about him and how, like him, many of us still spend our lives in our houses and out of them—Looking for home.